COLD T
A Sgt Major Cr
Book 2

By

Wendy Cartmell

© WENDY CARTMELL 2024

TABLE OF CONTENTS

By Wendy Cartmell

Wendy Cartmell is a bestselling Amazon author, well known for her chilling crime thrillers. These include the Sgt Major Crane mysteries, Crane and Anderson police procedurals, the Emma Harrison mysteries and a cozy mystery series, set in Muddlebay. Further, a psychic detective series has been written, the first of which, Touching the Dead has been followed by six further books in the series. Finally, the haunted series is a collection of ghostly happenings in buildings or objects.

Sgt Major Crane crime thrillers:
kindleunlimited

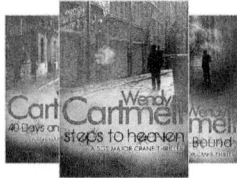

Crane and Anderson crime thrillers:
kindleunlimited

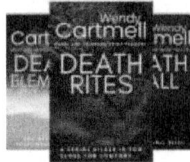

Emma Harrison mysteries
kindleunlimited

Supernatural suspense

Cozy mystery

Haunted houses

Cold Cases

COLD TIMES

When a good turn ends in murder…
Is it possible to have been murdered,
five years on from an assault?
When Owain Deans slips and falls at home and two days later
he is dead, the pathologist thinks so and contacts Sgt Major Crane.
It's now up to Crane. Can he really prove it was
murder, or will he be left with egg on his face.
And if it is murder, where the hell is the murderer?

FIVE YEARS AGO

CHAPTER 1

'Get a bloody move on!'

The shout rang around the range as Owain struggled through the mud, with his elbows helping to propel him forwards.

'Keep low. Do not raise your head.'

Owain Deans, his elbows and knees working in perfect harmony, crawling through the mud in a ditch in a so called 'exercise' would never do anything as stupid as lift his head. Not with all the bullets pinging overhead. He was steadfastly following the man in front when the dickhead suddenly stopped and Owain went straight into the bloke's boot, which smacked into his cheek bone.

'Do not stop!' rang out the voice. 'Keep crawling.'

'Come on, mate,' urged Owain. 'You're creating a bottleneck.' He was being pushed from behind and the grumbling of the men was threatening to spill over into anger from them, as well as from the instructor.

'I… I… can't.'

The man in front seemed terrified. Couldn't go forwards, couldn't go backwards. Frozen. Owain had to do something.

'It's okay,' he shouted. 'Come on, with me, dig those elbows in. That's it. Just one slither at a time. You can do it,' he urged as the man whose boots were in his face, managed to get moving again. 'Left, right, left, right,' Owain called, mimicking the man's movements himself. 'That's it, mate, you're doing well,' he urged, not knowing if the man in front had heard him.

Finally, they slithered down the slope, towards the end of the ditch, covered in mud from head to foot, but finally safe. They clambered up, and Owain pulled up his unfortunate colleague.

'Well done, mate,' Owain clapped the man on his back and wandered away to find his own unit.

'Deans!' the shout rang out. 'Over here – now!'

For fuck's sake, grumbled Owain to himself. What the hell does he want now? To be honest the thought of doing that crawl through the mud again, with bullets whizzing over his head which threatened to pummel him into the ground was terrifying. He was just too tired. But the Sgt Major had called his name. He had no choice but to go over.

'Sir?'

'Saw what you did there.'

Owain's cheeks flamed underneath their coating of mud. Here we go. He thought the worst.

'Well done. That's the sort of thing we like. Helping out without being asked. Coming to the aid of a mate in distress.'

Owain's face burst into a grin.

'Thank you, sir,' he stood proudly now, legs straight, back straight, shoulders back.

'Now fuck off back to barracks with the others. You stink to high heaven.'

'Yes, sir!' Owain shouted, saluted, then ran like the clappers.

CHAPTER 2

That evening, Owain Deans stood outside his newbuild two bedroomed terraced house. He was clean and dry and had had time to gulp a couple of pints with the lads at The Crimea. But he was tired and all he wanted was to get home and crawl into bed.

It was quite an achievement for a lowly squaddie to buy his own house. But to be fair, it had partly been paid for by a little money left to him by his grandparents. They had died as they had lived – together and frugally. Owain envied their love, and their togetherness. He wasn't married, wasn't even going out with anyone, the army was his life and his family. Pretty much all he needed for the immediate future.

He once again admired his house. The glow of the golden bricks, the small porch which served as protection for the front door and the fire-engine red of the door itself. He'd recently moved into the house but had quickly realised he'd need a lodger to help pay for it. He'd got the mortgage easily enough, but that wasn't the reality of the day to day running of a house. He'd advertised for a housemate and agreed that John Berry could move in, for a price of £400 per month, which would help enormously with the monthly bills.

Berry worked at Frimley Park Hospital, so Owain had figured he'd be okay as he had a responsible job. But what he hadn't banked on, was the bloke's behaviour when he was on his days off. Let's just say he liked to party. Anyway, they'd more or less rubbed along ok, probably because of Owain's job, which meant he wasn't there much. At such times Berry had the run of the house.

Owain hefted his kitbag on his shoulder and opened the front door. He'd just been on a 5 day exercise and was knackered. He was looking forward to a cup of tea. But that wasn't to be, as he walked in to find the house in total disarray. It seemed that Berry had had a party. There were cans, glasses, mugs, everywhere. Full ashtrays made the house smell disgusting, and the stink of weed was overwhelming in the kitchen.

Owain bunched his fists in anger. Being over six foot and all muscle from working out in the gym, he was a force to be reckoned with. He called Berry downstairs in a voice that would have impressed any Sgt Major.

'What the hell is all this?' he shouted when Berry appeared.

'Oh, yeah, right. Had a few friends over.'

'The mess is unbelievable, John. You've got to get rid of all this shit. I'm going upstairs to unpack and change my clothes and when I come down, I expect the house to be clean. If you keep doing this, you're out, do you hear me? It's about time you started to show some respect for me and for my home.'

Owain pushed past Berry, slamming him into the door frame and ran up the stairs, resisting the impulse to look in Berry's bedroom and the bathroom. He opened his bedroom door and dumped his kitbag on the floor. Looking around the room in the gloom, he saw the curtains were closed. He walked over and yanked them open, then turned to his bed and wondered why it was moving. It was as though there were animals under his duvet, making it roll around and look like it was boiling.

'What the fuck,' he yelled and pulled the duvet off the bed to find a naked, writhing couple, underneath.

The woman screamed and the man started shouting at Owain. 'Hey, what the hell do you think you're doing?'

'What I'm doing is getting you out of my fucking bed. Now piss off if you know what's good for you.'

As the couple scrambled off the bed, Owain scooped up their clothes, took two steps out of the bedroom and threw them over the banister and down the stairs.

'Get out of my bedroom and out of my house,' he yelled after them as they sprinted away from him.

Owain sat down on the bed, his head in his hands. It was no

good. John had to go. The only question was, when should he tell him. Just then he heard John calling for him.

He moved to the top of the stairs to see what the man wanted. As he started down the stairs, he saw John running up them, towards him, with a knife in his hand. Before Owain could react, John was stabbing him repeatedly in the stomach.

As Owain collapsed he heard a man ask, 'What the fuck have you done, John?'

Then a woman's voice saying 'Hello? We need an ambulance, someone's been stabbed.'

Looking down, Owain saw he was pushing his hand into his stomach and could see blood seeping through his fingers. Bloody hell it's me. I've been stabbed! Then the pain hit. Worse than anything he'd ever endured. His insides were on fire, and he couldn't think what to do. As he heard sirens, getting closer every second, he hoped to God they were for him, mumbled, 'Thank God,' and passed out.

CHAPTER 3

As he walked along the corridor in the Aldershot police station, which was as grey indoors as the pebbledash on the outside of the building, Detective Inspector Anderson read the file in his hands. He was in a typical concrete structure from the 1970's. A new station kept being promised by local officials, but so far there had been no movement on that score. And Anderson doubted there ever would be.

The file said that as a result of a 999-call last evening, the police were called to a house in the Ash Vale area, above Aldershot, which was shared by the victim, Owain Thomas Deans and the offender, John Berry.

The first officers to arrive found Owain slumped at the foot of the stairs bleeding heavily from knife wounds to his abdomen. John Berry was present, and he told the officers that he had stabbed Owain, and the knife was recovered.

Anderson looked through the viewing window of the room at the man sat at a table waiting to be interviewed. He was dishevelled, his skin pale grey, he was sweating, either from a hangover or fear - probably both. Derek had never had a clearer cut case than this. When arrested, John Berry had the victim's blood all over his hands, his fingerprints were all over the handle of the knife, which had the victim's blood on the blade. Oh yes, this was going to be a good one, thought Anderson as he barged through the door of the interview room, startling John Berry, just as he'd intended.

He pulled out a chair, allowing it to scrape along the floor. Once seated he patted the pockets of his tweed jacket, as if looking for his cigarettes, before remembering he didn't smoke. Nor were there any chocolate goodies, as he'd been put on a diet by his wife. Only then did he lift his face to the suspect sat opposite him.

John Bery was dressed in a paper suit, his clothes having been taken for forensic testing. A duty solicitor sat next to him, Mr Boult, looking bored. When the door opened and Detective Constable Brian Jones entered the room, Anderson could begin.

'Right, John,' said Anderson, 'the good news is that Owain is not dead.'

'Thank goodness,' mumbled John, not sounding in the least bit pleased.

'Oh, sorry, were you hoping he'd die?' snapped Anderson.

'Sorry,' mumbled John again.

The solicitor put his hand on his client's arm as if to tell him to shut up, but Berry shook it off.

'Anyway,' said Anderson, 'he's still unconscious and likely to be so for the next few days, so the doctors have told us. In the meantime, you are being charged with grievous bodily harm and when you go in front of the magistrates tomorrow, we'll be asking for you to be remanded to prison as we feel you'll do a runner.'

'Me?' John faked outrage.

Anderson just glared and John Berry was forced to slump back in his chair in acquiescence.

'So, this is your chance to tell us what happened last night,' said Anderson.

'No comment,' said Boult, once more laying his hand on Berry's arm.

As before Berry shook it off and said, 'Owain came back from exercise in a foul mood. He was shouting for me and seemed very angry. He was opening and closing his fists, you know? It was very intimidating, and I took a few steps backwards. I was afraid of him.'

'Where was this?'

'On the landing. I'd been in my bedroom when he came home, and I came out when he shouted for me.'

'Then what happened?' Anderson urged.

'Well, after shouting at me, he punched me in the face and

16

knocked off my glasses.'

'Mmm,' said Anderson, unconvinced, wondering why the man hadn't any bruises on his face, nor broken glasses, but decided to keep quiet about that.

'I picked myself up and ran at Owain, managing to barrel him out of the way, avoiding the kicks aimed at me. But then Owain dived into his bedroom and a moment later ran back out onto the landing with a dumb bell in his hand. Terrified, I ran back into my bedroom.'

Anderson nodded. 'I can understand that.'

'Mr Berry, I think that's enough for now,' intoned his solicitor.

But Berry ignored him and said, 'I took out a knife from my room and holding it at arm's length, I returned to the landing and told Owain to stay back. But Owain didn't listen, he lunged at me and fell onto the knife.'

'And that's your explanation, is it?' DC Jones asked.

'Yes, it is,' Berry said decisively.

'So did he fall on the knife several times in order to stab himself multiple times?' Anderson asked.

'Well, he must have done, mustn't he?'

Anderson motioned to DC Jones, 'Get him out of my sight, for God's sake, the Custody Sergeant is waiting for him.'

'Yes, Guv,' said DC Jones and moved to grab John Berry's arm at the elbow, yanking him up off his seat and dragging him towards the door.

Anderson was glad to get the weasel of a man out of the interview room. He was clearly lying through his teeth. Anderson had heard some stories in his time, but that one certainly took the biscuit. He shook his head and gathered up his papers, looking forward to a cup of tea and maybe a chocolate bar to go with it, as long as his wife didn't find out.

CHAPTER 4

Owain came round in Frimley Park Hospital with a blinding headache and his stomach on fire. 'What the fuck?' he muttered.

A nurse walking past heard him and went over to his bed.

'Hey, Owain, nice to meet you,' she said. 'We've waited a while for you to be back with us.'

Owain tried to move and winced with pain.

'It's ok, don't move, let me adjust the bed.'

Once his head was raised by the motorised bed and he could see her without lifting it, he asked, 'What day is it?'

'Wednesday.'

'When did I arrive?'

'Friday afternoon. By ambulance. You've sustained very serious stomach wounds I'm afraid and had a lifesaving operation. The doctor will be round later, and I'll get him to come and talk to you. For now, here have some water.'

'Any chance of any grub?'

'Best I can do is a cup of tea. Liquids only at the moment I'm afraid.'

As Owain's fantasy of a fry up dissolved, she bustled away.

When the doctor came, which seemed to be moments later, but the clock told him was two hours after the nurse had been, Owain wished he hadn't arrived, for he completely dispelled Owain's fantasies of a fry up, then or in the future.

And the future was something that Owain hadn't wanted to face either.

'Hi, Doc,' Owain said as the young man arrived, looking harassed, no doubt as a result of being over worked and under paid. 'So, when can I get back to work?' was what he really wanted to know. 'My regiment are due to move out next month.'

The doctor introduced himself as Alex Dorman, running a hand through his already dishevelled black hair, making it stand up and giving him the look of someone who'd just been electrocuted.

'Ah, Mr Deans, first of all let me say that you've sustained multiple stab wounds to the stomach.'

'Yes, with you so far, Doc,' said Owain, not knowing, or remembering the doctor's name. He was also wondering where this conversation was going. 'Hurts like a bugger at the moment, but I guess that will pass.'

'Well, yes, to a certain extent.'

'What? Sorry? When will this lot heal,' he said indicating his stomach, which was covered in substantial dressings, so Owain had no idea what was underneath them.

'I think it's best to talk to the consultant on his rounds tomorrow morning as to a definitive overview of the future for you. For now, as I say, multiple stab wounds, so I guess you won't be leaving us anytime soon.'

'Oh, fuck,' Owain said, slumping back on his pillows. 'I was hoping to be well enough to rejoin my regiment next month, I just told you we're moving out to take part in a huge exercise.'

'Exercise? Regiment?'

'Yes, I'm in the forces. British Army.'

'Ah, I understand. As I say, have a chat to the consultant in the morning. In the meantime, do as you're told and I'm sure you will be well on the road to recovery very soon.'

'But, Doc,' Owain called as the doctor bustled from the ward.

'Hello, you're awake again then,' said his nurse. 'More visitors if you're up to it?'

'Visitors?'

'Hello, Corporal Deans,' said a voice belonging to a man who strode up to his bed. 'DI Derek Anderson from Aldershot Police. I wonder if you could tell me what you remember of the incident.'

'That bastard,' Owain growled. 'Look what he did to me!'

'Indeed, sir, are you up to telling me about it.'

'Damn right, he's not going to get away with this!'

'You needn't worry on that score, Corporal,' said DI Anderson.

CHAPTER 5

After Owain had given his statement, which was the complete antithesis of John Berry's, he finished with, 'Then I woke up here and they won't even give me anything to eat.' He leaned back on his pillows, exhausted from the effort of telling Anderson what had happened.

Anderson thanked him and said, 'I'll be back to see you in due course, Mr Deans.'

As Anderson collected his coat, scarf, and trilby hat, Owain said, 'What the hell does that mean? Is John Berry going to pay for what he's done?'

'It means just what it says, sir. We'll go back and interview Mr Berry again, and then the CPS will decide how to move forward, and I'll come and tell you. Obviously, I'll interview you again, should I need to.'

Anderson then left before Owain could have another go at him. He went in search of the doctor who could lay out Deans' injuries and no doubt the nurses could supply him with a record of his medical intervention while in the hospital. What drugs he'd been given and such.

Sister Everhard gave him a copy of Owain's drug regime, which included intravenous antibiotics and morphine. 'He has a morphine pump at the moment, so he can give himself an extra shot as and when he needs it. But, of course, he can't overdose, as the machine is set to a maximum of so many grams allowed for his weight.'

As Anderson took the papers she handed him, she said, 'Oh, here's Dr Dorman. He can tell you more about Owain's injuries.'

'In plain English, if you don't mind, Sir,' said Anderson.

Sighing, Dr Dorman said, 'As a consequence of the assault, Owain Deans has sustained significant injuries. A section of his bowel had to be removed and he was required to have a catheter fitted which provided nutrition through a fine tube. As a result of these injuries, he will have to endure numerous surgical interventions, which will affect him both physically and mentally, I'm afraid. Is that clear enough for you?'

Ignoring the sarcasm, Anderson said, 'No more Army exercises for him, then.'

'No, in fact I'd be surprised if he is able to stay in. They will more than likely give him a medical discharge.'

Anderson grimaced, pretty sure that wouldn't go down well with Owain Deans.

CHAPTER 6

Once back at police headquarters, Anderson called for John Berry to be brought up to an interview room.

'Ah, John, there you are, just a quick chat if you don't mind.'

'I do actually, my brief's not here.'

'I'm not worried about that,' said Anderson. 'I just wanted to let you know that Owain is awake and talking and we've taken his preliminary statement.'

'Oh yeah? What's he been saying then.'

'Well, I'm afraid that his account of the incident is markedly different to yours. So, John Berry I am charging you with an offence contrary to Section 18 of the Offences Against the Person Act 1861. You do not have to say anything, but anything you do say may be used in evidence against you.'

'But it was self-defence,' John shouted as he was taken back to his cell. 'Why aren't you listening to me. I didn't do it on purpose, honest. Help! Let me go! I'm innocent!'

That last remark, made as John Berry was taken out of the interview room by a rather large, uniformed constable, made Anderson smile. That's what they all say, he thought, shaking his head. He'd heard it all before.

Back at his desk and picking up his phone, he called Aldershot Garrison, asking if he could speak to Padre Symmonds. Given his direct dial number, he once more made a call which the Padre answered. Given the details of the attack on Corporal Owain Deans, the Padre agreed immediately to call into the hospital and see his fellow soldier to see if he could offer both spiritual help, but also more formal help, dealing with the army authorities.

CHAPTER 7

Padre Symmonds looked at the figure in the hospital bed. He'd fallen asleep and looked more like a shrivelled human than a fighting fit member of the British Army. His weeks in hospital seemed to have stripped Owain of his bulk, leaving a bag of bones and a distended stomach where his injuries were plain to see, in a colostomy bag and feeding tube. The poor bloke would never be the same again.

He reached out and shook Owain awake. 'Come on, lad, it's time to get ready to leave. I've come to help you get dressed if you need me to.'

Owain shook off the Padre's hand. 'Fuck off. I'm fine. I can manage.'

The Padre nodded slowly, wondering that if Deans was able to dress himself on his own, why the hell hadn't he done so? But that wasn't very conciliatory, so instead said, 'Very well, Owain. I'll just lay out your clothes, then go and get a wheelchair.'

Owain grunted in reply. At least that suggestion hadn't been met with abuse, thought the Padre. Ducking down, he reached into Owain's locker by the side of his bed and took out rugby shirt, jeans, socks and trainers. He then pulled the curtains around Owain's bed and went in search of a wheelchair.

When he returned sometime later, having had to go all the way back down to reception, a doctor was with Owain telling him what to do with his feeding tube.

'Now Owain, here's a leaflet, but the basic procedure is, always use soap and water or alcohol-based hand sanitizer before you work with the tube. Make sure your hands are dry. You need to prevent clogs. This is one of the biggest problems with feeding tubes. Always flush your tube with the suggested amount of water before and after you use it, including when you use it to take meds. You'll need to flush it even on days you don't use it. Watch for infections. Keep the spot on your skin where the tube goes into your abdomen -- the stoma -- clean and dry. Check it every day for irritation, redness, swelling, or infection. Your GP may direct you to apply an antibacterial ointment after you clean the area. But in general, avoid using creams and powders around your stoma. Oh, and don't forget to care for your teeth and gums. Even if you get most or all your nutrition from a tube, your oral health is still important. Brush your teeth, gums, and tongue daily, and keep your lips moist with balm or petroleum jelly.'

'Oh joy,' the Padre heard Owain say, with a big dollop of sarcasm. But it didn't seem to stop the doctor.

'Now, obviously there will be some feeding tube side effects. You might have some discomfort or pain. Other possible side effects include irritation to the lining of your digestive tract; nausea, cramps, or stomach problems like diarrhoea or constipation; dehydration; infection at your surgical site; leakage from your stoma; a blockage of the tube; or even dislocation of the tube. If you get any trouble at all, please talk to your local doctor's surgery.'

'Are you serious?' queried Owain. 'Don't you know what it's like trying to get a doctor's appointment these days?'

'I know, Owain, but you have to try. I'm sure there will be several response options for you to use at your local surgery. They will have a copy of your notes as well, so the doctors will be able to pull up your medical history.'

As the doctor left, the Padre walked up to Owain's bed. He was glad to see the man was dressed, although a bit haphazardly. His top was pulled back to expose his stomach, he had no socks nor trainers on his feet and his jeans fly was open.

Owain must have seen him looking as he said, 'Can't get my socks and trainers on.'

'That's alright, here, I'll pop your slippers on, that'll be easier.'

Once that was done, and Owain had adjusted his clothing, the

Padre helped Owain into the wheelchair and handed him a rather large package to hold in his lap.

'Medication and stuff,' said Owain and the Padre was sure Owain's eyes filled with tears.

'Come on, let's get you home. Things always look better once you're back there.'

'Oh, God, what sort of shape is it in? It was a bloody mess when I last walked in.'

The Padre smiled. 'It's alright, it's all been taken care of,' and he began to push Owain out of the ward to the cries of goodbye and support from the staff.

Padre Symmonds didn't mention that it was his wife who'd gone in and done a deep clean of the house. She'd been horrified at the carnage when she'd gone in to get some supplies for Owain and promptly offered to sort it out before he came home.

What worried him was the support, or lack of it, that Owain would have at home now. Carers had been arranged to help him get up in the morning and get to bed in the evening, but the Padre was unsure what all this would mean to the man's mental health. When he'd come home from exercise a few weeks ago, he'd been a happy, healthy member of the British Army. Now he was broken, on medical leave and unlikely to recover fully. The prognosis wasn't positive.

CHAPTER 8

As the gates clanged behind him, John Berry had his first experience of prison. To be honest he was scared, but he'd never tell anyone that and was determined to act forcefully. The prison looked quite modern from the outside with a brick wall with a circular topping to dissuade climbers. There were five wings reaching out from a central circle. But that's where the modernism ended. Inside was all rust, damp, and there was a pervading air of depression. Everywhere you went you were accompanied by clanging metal, squeaking shoes and the tinkling of chains hanging from the prison officer's belts.

Prison. John Berry had never thought he would find himself in prison. So, okay, his behaviour could be a bit dodgy at times. Let's face it he wasn't Snow White. But then, who was? His over-riding thought kept playing on a loop: It was self-defence. I didn't do it on purpose, honest. Help! Let me go! I'm innocent!

But, of course, that attitude wouldn't work in prison, he quickly found. A bloke in front of him in the queue for processing upon their arrival, kept going on like that and was quickly put in his place by the prison officers and by the other members of the day's intake.

'Shut your face!' one shouted.

'Stop moaning, or you'll find your teeth down your throat!'

'Prick,' was succinct and to the point, John thought, as he watched the poor bloke being elbowed in the stomach and staggering with pain.

John knew he wasn't the most handsome of men, and in fact looked more like a weasel than an adonis, but he was happy with the facial features he had and wanted to keep them intact. So, a complete change of attitude was called for.

He was on B Wing inside Winchester prison, the biggest wing, mainly for remand prisoners. It was too cold at night and too hot by day. At first, he was in a cell on his own, but was soon moved into a two-man cell, due to pressure on accommodation, or some such bollocks.

John settled in by firstly saying he was there for grievous bodily harm to anyone who would listen and told everyone they better keep away from him, or they'd get a taste of his fists. That seemed to work, and he continued to tell anyone who would listen, to be afraid of him. He started lifting weights, as going to the gym got you out of your cell and helped with his physique, which wasn't great, but gradually improved.

They were setting up an education wing, but Berry didn't have much interest in that. He already had a medical career, (well alright, he'd only been a hospital porter) so was used to steady employment. However, he found that there were low expectations and apathy among staff and prisoners. Difficulties with recruitment and retention meant that there were not enough staff to offer even the most basic regime, consistently. But John knew he had to tough it out until his trial. He then hoped he'd be sent to a different prison, as conditions on C wing (for those prisoners who had been found guilty and sentenced) was in short, truly horrendous, if the gossip was to be believed. And John saw no reason why it wouldn't be true. There he'd be locked in his cell for 23 hours a day. That would either be on his own, or sharing with another prisoner, neither scenario very delectable.

Then he got details of his trial, and his legal aid lawyer visited him in prison.

Jason Boult was tall, thin and gangly with a large Adam's apple that John couldn't take his eyes off. The man also swallowed a lot, which made it even more watchable.

'So, John, you're up for trial in a couple of weeks. How are you feeling about that?'

'I just want it over with, to be honest, Mr Boult.'

'We're anticipating a guilty verdict you know. You did stab

Owain Deans, after all.'

'Yeah, I know. I've been thinking about that.'

'Oh yes?' the solicitor looked up from his notebook.

'Perhaps I ought to plead guilty. Do you think I'll get a shorter sentence if I do?'

'I think that is highly likely, John. The courts always look kindly on those saving them money and I'm sure I could agree a reduced sentence recommendation from the prosecution.'

Berry thought about it, whilst chewing on his thumb nail, also well aware that Mr Boult would appreciate a short trial that he wouldn't have to prepare for, and then said, 'Alright, Mr Boult, let's do it. I'll plead guilty.'

CHAPTER 9

Berry was taken from Winchester Prison to Winchester Crown Court. He was jolted along in the prison transport, which was a white truck, kitted out like an armoured vehicle with small windows that were blacked out and separate 'slots' for the prisoners to sit in. John sat there in a suit his mother had bought for him, with his hands in handcuffs, trying not to throw up. His hands were shaking, and sweat sheened on his face. But there was no compassion from the prison guards who roughly pulled him up out of his seat and bundled him out of the van.

After a short while down in the cells below the court, John was once more pulled out of one seat and plonked in another in the courtroom, while they waited for the Judge. He could see his solicitor, Mr Boult, who turned and gave him a smile of encouragement. But John couldn't smile in return. His face was frozen. Fear in his eyes. Words dying on his lips.

The prosecution solicitor leaned over to Mr Boult, and they had a whispered conversation. John nearly threw up there and then! What were they talking about? Had the deal gone sour? Fuck, he shouted in his mind, over and over again.

And then the Judge was there, sweeping in like a black crow. John was pulled out of his anxiety attack and had to concentrate. Once everyone had stood, including the clerk to the court and the transcript officer, and then sat down again, the judge peered over his half glasses at John as the clerk to the court read out the charge of grievous bodily harm (GBH).

His solicitor had explained that GBH was a term used for major injuries like deep lacerations, broken bones, or concussions. Those injuries that had the potential to be life-altering and so had a more severe maximum punishment of up to life imprisonment. And whichever way you looked at it, John thought, Owain's life had really been altered as a direct result of being stabbed in the stomach.

Then someone asked him, 'How do you plead?'

Licking his dry lips with a sandpaper tongue, John said, 'Guilty.'

'Very well,' the Judge intoned, 'We'll move straight along to sentencing. Is Mr Deans in court?'

'Yes, your honour,' said the prosecution barrister.

'Would he like to give evidence to give us some context as to the extent of his injuries and how his life has been changed?'

'He would, indeed, your honour.'

'Very well, have him come forward.'

CHAPTER 10

Owain Dean's wheelchair had a squeaky wheel. As he slowly pushed himself along the length of the courtroom, the squeak became louder and louder, the nearer he got to the front. John shivered. This would be the first time he'd faced Owain since the incident, as he called it in his mind.

Owain stopped his chair and looked in horror at the witness box. John closed his eyes. There was no way Owain could get up there and John could see his friend's face flush with embarrassed anger.

'Please stop by the prosecution table, Mr Deans, that will be fine,' the Judge said.

Owain gave a taut nod.

'Now I wonder, could you tell me in your own words what your life is like now? Since the incident, that is.'

It seemed the very thought of what had happened filled Owain with anger, as his fists balled and his neck muscles stood out.

He ground out the words, 'Well, your honour, I've lost everything. My livelihood, as I've been invalided out of the army. And, of course, the Marines were my life. The British Army was my family. I will find it difficult to get work. I'm trying to re-train for a job that I could do sitting down, but I get brain fog because of the constant pain I'm in and the medication I have to take and am finding studying very difficult, if not impossible. I can no longer eat, as I can't absorb nutrition from food anymore and need a feeding tube. And this is all because of a good deed,' Owain's voice was getting louder. 'From giving someone down on his luck a room at a reasonable rent, to being in a wheelchair and losing everything, inside six months. Ha! It beggars belief. So, your honour, I feel I've lost everything. I'm hoping to keep my house as my benefits will pay for it, but beyond that... I've nothing.

'When you can't eat the same way as everyone else, it changes your social life and makes you feel left out. I miss the taste of food and drinking cider. I also feel self-conscious about my tube and my stoma. I had to rethink how I do everyday things like eating out and travelling. It's all so difficult that I'm not bothering anymore.'

Owain dropped his head, tears falling on his lap.

'Thank you, Mr Deans,' said his Honour. 'You may step – sorry, leave, um, thank you.'

John closed his eyes against the embarrassment of both his Honour and Owain Deans. He felt like throwing up. He daren't breathe. If he didn't move, perhaps everything would go away. Fade like a mirage on the horizon in a desert. He wanted to turn back time.

But of course, he couldn't, and when he didn't respond to the judge asking him to stand, a prison officer grabbed him by his arm and roughly pulled him up.

John couldn't look at the Judge and hung his head in supplication.

'John Berry, I sentence you to eight years imprisonment. Take him down.'

And with that it was over. The next eight years of his life taken from him, just as he'd taken part of Owain's stomach. That was the price he had to pay. He'd taken a pound of flesh from Owain, and it felt as though the judge had just stripped a pound of flesh from his own bones in return.

CHAPTER 11

Kim knocked at the door, to be greeted with, 'Come in the door's open.'

'Hi, Owain,' she called from the hall. 'I'm Kim Symmonds, the Padre's wife.'

'Get in here then,' a gruff voice said. 'It's easier if you come to me than the other way round.'

Kim pushed open the door to what she assumed was the lounge. She saw Owain Deans with his feet up on the settee, surrounded by the remains of a meal.

'Owain?' she said suspiciously, as she thought the man couldn't get any nutrition from food and would do serious damage to his insides if he attempted to eat.

'It's alright,' he grumbled. 'I didn't really eat it. I just wanted the taste of it in my mouth more than anything. Want some?' and he pushed a pizza box towards her.

'No, you're alright,' she said. 'Can I get you anything? Do anything for you?'

'Na, not really, I'm alright, I guess.'

But Kim seriously doubted that. 'Do you want to talk about it? About what happened and how you're feeling now?'

'What the hell's the point?'

Then she saw the scissors. 'Owain, what have you done?'

'What?' he frowned. Then saw where she was pointing. 'Oh that. I'm fed up with it already, bastard thing just gets in the way and hurts like a bugger if I catch it by mistake.'

Kim could see now that Owain had cut the line and therefore would not be able to feed himself. He would slowly starve to death. Instead of pointing that out, she pulled out her phone. Turning and walking away she spoke into her phone, before returning to the room.

'So, anyway what's it to you, what I do?' he demanded.

'I want to try and help, that's all. Be a friendly face. Everyone needs a friend, don't they?'

'I wouldn't choose you.'

'Why not? I'm ex-army too.'

'You are?' that seemed to change his attitude.

As they talked, she persuaded him to be reconnected to the equipment that provided the intravenous nutrition. 'I sent for an ambulance,' she told him.

'Ambulance, what the hell for?'

'Because the line now needs replacing, Owain. We can't just stick it back together you know,' she said, smiling to take the sting from her words.

'I've fucked up,' he said, as an ambulance pulled up outside.

'You could say that.' She grinned and moved to open the door to the crew, who would get him in the ambulance and take him back into hospital.

As she stood by her car, watching the ambulance disappear into the distance, she wondered if cutting the Hickman line had been a cry for help. Owain needed company and fussing over, to make him feel wanted, important, not just a bloke in a wheelchair. Kim shook her head. She couldn't even imagine what he'd been through, psychologically, emotionally and physically. She'd left the army for love, but it still hurt, that pang when she saw the soldiers out and about on the garrison. When they filled the pews for a service. And she'd readily made that decision. It hadn't been thrust on her like it had for Owain. It was no wonder he lost the plot at times.

CHAPTER 12

'Hi Owain,' Nurse Molly Brown shouted as she pushed open the door to Owain Dean's house.

As she put her head around the door to the lounge, Owain snarled, 'What the fuck do you want?'

Taken aback, but determined to battle through, Molly, said, 'I have come to check your line and change the dressings on your stomach. You need to keep it clean you know, as you've had a new line inserted and you'll need a dressing on it for the next couple of weeks.'

'I'm not interested,' he said, turning up the volume on the television.

Calmly taking the remote from him she turned off the tv and put the remote out of his reach.

'Oy, what do you think you're doing?' he roared.

'I've just told you, Owain, helping you. I'm here to change your dressings, not to be drowned out by the television. Now come on, lift your sweatshirt so I can get on.'

'Fuck off.'

Molly's patience was definitely being tested. 'Come on, Owain, the sooner you let me change your dressings, the sooner I'll be out of your hair.'

As Molly reached for Owain, he lashed out, hitting her face and knocking her glasses off. Stunned, she stopped reaching for him. Took a step backwards and searched for her glasses. Finding them, she put them on, noting that they were wonky and that one arm was hanging off. For God's sake, she thought. I've had enough of this.

'Alright, you win,' she said and went to collect her case.

'Where you off to?' he said.

'Pardon?' Molly couldn't believe what she's just heard.

'Aren't you changing my dressings?'

'Not a chance,' she said, holding onto her glasses. 'I'm never coming here again. I didn't study for all those years to be treated like this. I won't ever see you again, because I'll never come here again. I'm withdrawing my services. Goodbye.'

Even though she wanted to shout and swear at him, she was proud of her restraint. The last thing she needed was for Owain to complain about her. Holding onto her glasses with one hand and her case with the other, she made a swift exit.

**

It was a couple of days later when Molly saw Kim Symmonds at the surgery. She told her what had happened at Owain's house, and that the surgery had made the decision to withdraw nursing services.

'I won't go to see him again. I'm sorry Kim but I can't have that. Be treated in that way and being hit. My glasses have been replaced by the surgery, thank goodness as I couldn't afford to replace them.'

'No that's quite alright, I do understand,' Kim said. 'No one deserves to be subjected to that sort of abuse.'

But it troubled Kim. She wasn't sure what she could do to help Owain if he kept behaving like that.

CHAPTER 13

Owain was in his usual place on the sofa, when his mobile rang. It was Frimley Park Hospital. 'Hello, is that Owain Deans?'

'Yes,' he grunted.

'It's Frimley Park Hospital Outpatients Department. Why didn't you come in for your check up yesterday?'

'Didn't feel good.'

'It's very important that you do, you know. We need to keep a look out for –'

'Fuck off.'

'I'm sorry?'

'You heard. I'm not interested.' Owain's voice was raising in volume.

'But Mr Deans you need to be checked regularly Your Hickman line –'

'My line is fine, but I can't be doing coming into hospital it's a waste of my time and to be honest too much bloody effort. Now why don't you all leave me alone!' he snarled at the top of his voice, and then threw his mobile phone against the wall. Followed by a glass vase he never used. A paperweight similarly unwanted was next. Then he got rid of three mugs. As he watched the destruction, old coffee and tea dripped down the wall and the floor was a mess of glass and crockery.

At that point the doorbell rang.

'Fuck off,' he yelled.

But instead of obeying the instruction, whoever was there ignored him and pushed open the door anyway. Then into the room stepped Padre Symmonds.

'What the fuck do you want?' Owain yelled.

'Hello, Owain. Just thought I'd see how you're doing.'

'Don't give me that crap. Who rang you? The doctors? The hospital?'

'Your neighbours, actually. They are really concerned about you.'

'Not concerned enough to ring the doorbell.'

'That's not surprising, the shouting they can hear and the smashing of things.'

'Oh.' Owain was beginning to calm down. He had to admit it was exhausting being so angry all the time. But he wasn't about to tell Padre Symmonds that.

'Look, Owain, I know you're feeling rotten, but if you don't keep up your hospital appointments then you're going to feel worse.'

'That's not possible. I feel like crap all the time now.'

'Well maybe you'd feel better if you did go.'

'Yeah, but that hospital transport takes forever, and I can be there hours when I don't need to be,' Owain sulked.

'Look, how about if I get you a volunteer to drive you, would you go then?'

Owain looked a bit brighter. 'Yeah, yeah, I might.'

'And what about the house?'

'What about it,' said Owain, but privately wondering what the interfering old fart was going on about now.

'Well, I'm concerned about the house. The state it's in. Do you have a cleaner?'

'My sister-in-law comes in from time to time.'

'What about your brother?'

'What about him? I think he prefers to pretend I don't exist.'

'I'm sure that isn't true. Maybe he's having a hard time dealing with it all.'

'He's having a hard time? What the fuck? I'm the one that was stabbed. Not him. No, he's just a selfish arsehole who doesn't think of anyone but himself. I think he's ashamed of me. So, fuck him.'

'Of course, I'm sorry, Owain, but you can help yourself you know. Give yourself a better quality of life by following the medical advice. You still have a lot to live for, you've just got to find it and try and turn things around. You don't need to live like this. Do you have the money for care?'

'Yes. I got some of that criminal compensation money.'

'Well then spend some of it on your actual care. You have a lovely home here and it deserves to be clean and nice.'

Thank God the Padre left after that sanctimonious speech, but Owain had the satisfaction of throwing a plate at the door as the Padre closed it behind him.

PRESENT DAY
CHAPTER 14

The sound of the telephone awoke Padre Symmonds from a deep slumber. He was on a winter break and just about to ski down the green run when someone knocked into him. He fell splat onto the snow, but wondered why it was packed so hard. And where had that wintery wind come from, a moment ago it had been dazzling sunshine!

It took the Padre a few seconds to realise that he was no longer in his dream, but on the floor in just a pair of boxer shorts and the heating wasn't on. He shook his head and clambered back onto the bed, to find his mobile was buzzing all over the top of the bedside cabinet.

'Symmonds,' he grunted.

'Ah, Padre,' said a voice he didn't recognise. 'We have a problem you might be able to help us with.'

'Yes?' Francis Symmonds shook his head to clear the cobwebs.

'It's Owain Deans, one of your flock.'

'Ex-flock you mean.'

'Exactly and that's the trouble. He's all over the place, Padre. Shouting and throwing stuff out of the window at unsuspecting passers-by. I understand that he won't take his medication and his mental health is suffering as a result of his injuries.'

'And being chucked out of the army won't have helped.'

'Exactly, I knew you'd understand. Can you call round?'

'Of course, I'll get my diary and get back to you.'

'I don't think you understand, Padre. He needs talking down

now. If you can't come, I'll have to wade in and arrest him.'

'Bloody hell, alright, alright, but it's Kim you want. She's on her way.'

After closing the call, Francis dug Kim in the ribs and told her about Owain.

***

Kim rolled out of bed and danced around the room, grabbing whatever she could find to wear. It was a pair of joggers and hoodie that she'd had on last night. Grabbing a bottle of water from the kitchen, she fished her car keys out of the bowl on the hall table and opened the door, to find a world of dazzling cold white. Owain Deans had a lot to answer for, for dragging her out this early in the morning.

She was at the ex-marine's house inside 10 minutes, to find two police cars and a straggling gaggle of rubberneckers. Empty cider cans kept being lobbed out of the window of Owain's house and a stream of rhetoric was shouted at the top of his voice.

'Fuck the lot of you! Fuck the army! Fuck John Berry! You've all ruined my life! I can't take anymore! I'd be better off dead!'

'Owain, it's Kim Symmonds here, I'm coming in.'

'Are you sure, Kim?' said Sgt Bevins. 'Oh, and thanks for coming.'

'Owain's more bluster than anything. He'd never hurt me I'm certain of that. I've been working with him on coming to terms with his life and living with his injuries.'

'With respect, it's not working at the moment!'

Kim had to laugh. 'Not surprising, judging by the number of empty cider cans!'

'I'm behind you,' Bevins said. 'You're not going in otherwise.'

'If you insist,' she said, moving off towards the front door. Once there, she realised it was unlocked as she pushed down the handle. Easing open the door, she called, 'Owain, it's Kim. I'm coming in.'

She turned to Bevins, shushing him, so he didn't set Owain off by announcing the police presence in his house.

As she turned into the lounge, Owain could be seen throwing cans out of the open window, sat in his wheelchair. His clothes were filthy, as was he. His hair had grown and was matted and greasy. His tee-shirt was stained, as were his track suit bottoms. His eyes were wild, and he was wincing with pain.

'Get an ambulance here,' Kim whispered to Bevins, as Owain burst into a fit of coughing that seemed to be coming from the very bottom of his lungs. A smoker's cough, rattling nails.

Bevins nodded and spoke into his radio.

As he was doing that Kim walked into the room. 'Hey, Owain, how are you doing?'

'What?' his head whipped round. 'Oh, it's you. What the hell do you want?'

Kim smiled. 'Why to help you, of course. Look it's freezing in here, you're shivering. Shall we close the window, and you can tell me what's bothering you.'

'What's bothering me? Are you mad? You know what's bothering me.' Spittal fell from his lips, covering his legs in small bubbles.

She nodded. 'But this isn't the way to deal with it, is it Owain? We've talked about this before.'

Owain hung his head for a moment, and then looked up at Kim. The pain in his eyes made her want to cry. He was such a tortured soul. He hadn't deserved those injuries and to lose everything.

'Let's get you warm, shall we?' she said as she grabbed a throw off the settee, wrapping him in it as Bevins closed the window.

'I'm sorry,' Owain sobbed. 'I feel so ill. It's just so awful and so unfair.'

'I know,' she soothed.

'Whatever happened to the man I used to be?' he cried.

But neither Kim, nor Bevins had an answer for him.

CHAPTER 15

'Giles, where's your brother?'

'And hello to you too, mother.'

'Oh, for goodness sake, grow up. Now where is Owain?'

'How the hell do I know? Isn't he at home? He's always at home!'

'Giles, I'm here in Wales. You're in Frimley, a few measly miles from your brother. Can't you call in and see how he is?'

'But mum it's Saturday...'

'Exactly so you're not at work. Call me in an hour and let me know what's going on.'

With that, she put the phone down on his protests.

Giles Deans was fed up with his bloody brother, although he could never admit that to his mother.

'Who was that?' called his wife, Sheila.

'Mother.'

She laughed. 'You off then? Off to check on Owain?'

'Yeah,' he said as he shuffled into the kitchen in his slippers. 'Have you seen my trainers?'

'By the front door. Keep me posted, won't you?' she called after him.

He quickly changed into his trainers. He already had on jeans and a polo shirt, so pulled on his wax jacket over the top. Opening the door, he was thinking, bloody mother, bloody brother. He was thoroughly fed up with both of them. It had been five years since Owain had been attacked and it wasn't just Owain who was suffering. The whole family had been dragged under by it all. His mum had aged 10 years. His dad now had dementia. He didn't know how his wife put up with it all with such good humour. Although she did admit she enjoyed the few hours alone, when he had to run off to see Owain.

Within 20 minutes he was pulling up outside Owain's home. Climbing out of the car he saw the once proud red front door was faded and the net curtains looked more like grey cobwebs. It was sad, as the whole place had an air of neglect, including his brother himself.

He rang the doorbell but got no response. He banged on the door but got no response. Bloody hell. 'Owain!' he shouted. 'Open the bloody door!'

His fist was raised to bang on the door again, when a head poked out of next door.

'He's not here.'

'What? Where the hell is he then? He never goes anywhere.'

'Try Frimley Park Hospital. They took him away a couple of days ago. He'd banged his head or some such,' and then the head disappeared, and the door slammed shut.

'Shit, shit, shit, shit!' was all Giles could say. Why hadn't they known? Why hadn't anyone called them?

He raced back to Frimley in his car and managed to find a space in the hospital car park. Striding through the main entrance, he enquired at the desk as to the location of his brother. He was surprised to find he was directed to the High Dependency Unit.

When a nurse answered his buzzer at the entrance to the ward, he asked after his brother, Owain Deans.

'Oh, thank goodness,' she said. 'We didn't know if poor Owain had any family, and if he did, how to get hold of you. When he was admitted he didn't have a mobile on him. And there were no family details on his medical records.'

'Why didn't he just tell you about us?' Giles thought it all very odd.

'Because he was brought in unconscious with a head injury,' she explained. 'And I'm very sorry, but he's not recovered, and he's not expected to survive.'

'From banging his head?' Giles thought this all very strange. It must have been a bad bang.

'No, from sepsis,' she explained. 'His whole stomach is now

infected and we're losing the battle. The antibiotics can't touch it. If you'll just wait there, I'll check that you can see him.'

Giles stumbled into a chair. Unconscious? Not expected to survive? Dear God, how was he going to tell his mother? He fumbled in his pocket to call Sheila, but the nurse reappeared.

'Follow me,' she said so quietly he wasn't sure she'd spoken.

He followed her almost silent footsteps to the last bed on the ward. In it, his large, strapping brother, former Marine, lay shrivelled in the middle of the bed. His breathing was ragged, his eyes closed. When Giles touched him, there was no response. Nothing at all.

Giles held his brother, leaning awkwardly over the bed. But he wanted Owain to know that someone was there with him. That Giles had come. That he cared. Then he realised that he was actually holding Owain for purely selfish reasons. Not having done enough for his brother in life, he could try and offer some comfort in death, to salve his own despair.

Then Owain moved slightly, tried to catch his breath and failed. There was the faintest of sighs, then nothing.

Giles shivered as his brother died and it seemed as though Owain's spirit moved through Giles, before fading away into the ether.

CHAPTER 16

'Right, Jack, let's get on with it. Who's next?' Major Martin said, stood by an empty examination table in the morgue at Frimley Park Hospital. The Major was known as 'the Michelin Man', due to his rotund appearance when in his crime scene suit. Today he was dressed in scrubs with a plastic apron over them. Lately he'd been concerned by his hair loss, and so had shaved his head, giving him the polished bowling ball look. But he was nearing retirement and had never much bothered about his appearance.

'Just coming,' called his assistant, pushing over a trolley, on which lay the naked corpse of their next patient, covered by a white sheet.

The two men manhandled the dead man onto the metal table.

'So, who's this?' the Major asked.

'Owain Deans, aged 35, admitted to hospital with sepsis and a head injury, but he died two days later without regaining consciousness.'

Major Martin removed the sheet and tried hard not to recoil. 'Goodness me, what a bloody mess!'

The corpse in front of him had several unhealed wounds in his stomach.

'Stab wounds?' he asked Jack.

'Yes, according to his medical records he was attacked with a knife in his own home five years ago and has had a bloody awful time of it since.'

Major Martin could see Owain had a Hickman Line inserted. Grabbing the paperwork Jack held out to him, it confirmed to the Major that Owain had been unable to absorb nutrients from food since his attack and subsequent operations over the past five years, so he had to have a tube inserted directly into his stomach. The Major surmised that that would more than likely be the source of the sepsis.

'Hells bells he's been in the wars, hasn't he.'

Jack nodded. 'Literally. According to this he's ex-military. Sustained the injuries while he was serving near here in Aldershot.'

'In that case, call Sgt Major Crane over at Provost Barracks would you? I reckon he's going to be interested in this one. I've heard he's back working with Billy Williams.'

'Really? Contact the Military police?'

'Oh, absolutely, Jack. This bloke was murdered.'

'By sepsis?' said Jack. 'I know I'm still in training, but how on earth do you get murdered by sepsis?'

***

That was precisely what Sgt Major Crane said when he got to the morgue. 'How do you get murdered by sepsis?'

'And hello to you too!'

'Sorry, Major, good afternoon. So, how do you get murdered by sepsis?'

'By looking at what got him into this state,' said Major Martin. 'Come over here and see.' The Major led Crane over to an examination table and took away the sheet covering the body.

Crane whistled at the sight of the man's injuries. It was clear the man had been stabbed previously from the red scars peppering his stomach and the open sores.

'Meet Corporal Owain Deans,' continued Major Martin. 'He was involved in a fight at his home, apparently, some years ago, and his lodger stabbed him in the stomach with a knife several times. He lost half his stomach and had to endure multiple operations.'

'Mmm,' said Crane. 'It wasn't one of my cases, but I can pull out the file when I get back.'

'I'll send you everything I have once I've written up the postmortem, but I'll also lodge it with the Coroner, of course. The investigation will hinge on showing a causal link between the knife attack and then the death by sepsis. So that means it's over to you, Crane.'

Joy oh joy thought Crane, as he left to return to Provost Barracks on Aldershot Garrison. As he went down to the car park the squally rain threw a particularly vicious downpour at him, the cold drops like needles on the skin of his face. They caught in his short black hair that now had several sections of grey in it and lodged in his beard, grown all those years ago to try and hide the shrapnel scar running down his cheek.

He found his car, an Audi coupe automatic because of his gammy leg. The injury didn't bother him so much anymore, but driving a manual car irritated it so much, it was not worth it. He rarely needed a stick, but always kept one in the car, as he never knew when it would come in handy.

He climbed in and as he pulled out of the car park, he wondered how Owain Deans had felt at being invalided out of the army. If he was anything like Crane, he'd not had a good time of it. Crane's saviour had been working with DI Anderson for the Aldershot police, and he wondered if there had been anything in place to save Owain from the desperation of a life changing injury.

CHAPTER 17

Crane was at his desk in Provost Barracks when HM Coroner referred the matter to the military police to take operational control of the new investigation. He read the memo which told him he had to immediately commence an investigation to establish any causal link between the original assault and Mr Dean's death some five years later. It was felt the cause of death was septicaemia, which was a consequence of an infected Hickman line being used to treat chronic intestinal failure due to previous abdominal trauma and surgery.

The Coroner had further stated that, based on the information available, there was strong clinical and pathological evidence that the abdominal injuries sustained by Mr Deans made a significant contribution to his death five years later.

Crane printed off the memo and walked to Billy's office. Of course, Crane had known the case was coming from Major Martin and also Billy. Everyone was citing pressure of work as to why they couldn't do it. Aldershot police. Billy himself. And so, it was going to be left to their cold case expert, as Billy had put it. The other thing Billy had called him was an independent investigator. Which he guessed was about right. He didn't have any authority within either the police, or the military. Which should help calm the family, who, it appeared, had been traumatised by the whole event. And who could blame them?

'Got the memo,' Crane said, as Billy looked up from his desk.

'Deans?'

Crane nodded.

Billy said, 'The investigative challenge of proving an unlawful assault is clearly not an issue. Berry had been found guilty of the original assault and had served half of his eight-year sentence. The challenge now is to ensure that Owain Deans' family receive the support and reassurance that a full investigation will be conducted, and that all information will be analysed and tested appropriately.'

'So where is he?' Crane asked.

'Who?'

'John Berry, the man who stabbed Owain Deans.'

'Ah.'

'Ah? Ah what?'

'We don't actually know.'

'You mean the police have lost him?'

'Mmm, you could put it that way,' said Billy bashfully. 'Or it could be the Probation Service's fault. But finding people is kind of your speciality, Crane.'

'Mmm,' Crane grumbled and went over to Dudley-Jones, who, as usual was hidden behind his computer screens, plural. Why he needed more than one, Crane wasn't at all sure. But then he wasn't a computer expert.

'Who have you lost?' Dudley-Jones asked.

'John Berry. Here's the details. Skipped probation after being released from prison.'

'Okay, I'll see what I can do.'

Confident Dudley-Jones was on the case, Crane sloped off to grab a coffee. He was going to need the caffeine as he wrote a list of things to do. He had a feeling it was going to be a very long list.

CHAPTER 18

Crane sat scratching his head. He knew he needed a list of things to do, but to be honest lists weren't really his thing. Yet he knew that without one he'd never keep track of all the things he had to do. No longer with a dedicated team, he decided to pull together a temporary team. He looked at the notebook in front of him and the pen in his hand. That would never do. It just wouldn't work. It was time for his whiteboard. Going to the wall of Billy's office he cleaned the board of the previous investigation notes. The pictures and maps had long gone, there were just some random scribblings left.

And so armed with his board he began.

The Deans Family. Crane wondered if Kim Symmonds would meet the family with him. She'd helped when Deans had first come out of hospital and been an on/off counsellor for him until his death. She would also be a good source of information as to his mental state both for Crane and for his family.

He needed to recover the original prosecution file and unused material. He noted down Military police and civilian police files. Prosecution and defence solicitors' files. To include recovery of original exhibits.

Locating John Berry was the co-opted job of Dudley Jones.

Crane needed to find the couple who had called the ambulance on the night Deans was stabbed. Again Dudley-Jones to assist.

Pathology and establishing a clear causal link – he'd work with Major Martin on that one.

He also made a note to investigate other expert advisers and witnesses that could aid his case.

Standing back, he was pleased with his efforts. He also added photographs of Deans, one after the stabbing and one after death. Also, a photograph of John Berry.

Would his efforts be enough, though, he wondered? He would give it his best shot, after all Owain Deans deserved justice. Four years for ruining a person's life and then for the original attack to effectively kill Deans, wasn't fair as far as Crane was concerned and he was sure Owain Deans would feel the same. It was up to Crane, Dudley-Jones and Kim to give the ex-marine the justice he deserved. Deans had been one of their own. He deserved the best job they could do.

CHAPTER 19

'I really appreciate this, you know,' Crane said to Kim as they stood outside Giles Deans' house in Frimley. His mother was also there, visiting from Wales, he understood.

'It's fine, it's my job now, you know, being a counsellor. And it keeps me out from under Francis' feet,' she smiled.

Kim had been Crane's office manager, back in the day, before she'd left the service to marry Padre Symmonds and re-train as a counsellor. Then her dress was her severe uniform, with hair pulled back into a sharp bun. Now, she was all soft lines, with soft fabric trousers and blouses. Her hair was short and tousled, but Crane knew the army attention to detail was still there, below the surface, meaning her reports would be detailed and complete.

'And anyway,' she finished, 'you'll be getting my invoices don't forget!' and with that, she rang the doorbell. 'How much do they know?' she hissed.

'Not a lot,' Crane had to confess.

'Best start from scratch then,' she said as the door was opened.

'Hello, I'm Clive Deans,' the man said. 'You must be?'

'Sgt Major Crane and Kim Symmonds.'

'Exactly. Come in then,' and he turned and walked away leaving the door open.

Crane and Kim followed him into a large living/dining/kitchen, filled with loads of light. It actually made Crane squint against the sun. His own Victorian in Ash had smaller individual rooms, nothing like this modern box.

Clive was pretty keen to get started and as soon as they sat, said, 'Well?'

'Well, Mr Deans?' asked Kim.

'Well, why are you both here? We know he's dead, what else is there to know?'

'Clive!' shouted an older woman, white hair thinning so badly it was barely there. Clothes as loud as her voice and on the large side. 'Don't be so rude.'

'Sorry, mother, but it's all such a strain!'

Clive Deans indeed did look flustered, he was sweaty and dishevelled, so much so that Crane wondered what he was on. Drugs? Or more likely vodka.

'Kendra Deans,' Owain's mother introduced herself.

'Good morning, I'm Penny, Clive's wife. Can I get you anything? Tea? Coffee?' she asked, already halfway out of her seat.

'No, we're fine, thank you,' said Kim.

Penny nodded, a petite woman with her swinging bobbed hair held back by a hairband, and sat back down.

'So, how can we help you, Mr Crane,' Mrs Deans said.

'Sgt Major,' hissed Clive.

'It's fine,' Crane waved it away.

'First of all,' said Kim, 'please accept our condolences on the death of Owain.'

'Thank you,' his mother said. 'Although it wasn't altogether a shock. Not considering what he'd been through.'

'No indeed.'

'The thing is,' said Crane, 'the pathologist strongly feels that as Owain's death is so closely related to his injuries, that there is a case to believe that his death was...' Crane paused. 'Was murder.' There. He'd said it. Thrown a rock in the pond. He watched the ripples spread.

Penny went 'Oh!' and put her hand over her mouth.

Mrs Deans looked like she was going to faint.

It was Clive who seemed to get it. 'So, John Berry is going to be charged with murder,' he said.

Crane nodded. 'Absolutely right, Mr Deans. That is the plan.'

'But there is a lot of work to be done before then,' cautioned Kim. 'Both by Sgt Major Crane here, the police, the CPS and you, the family. I will work with you, and keep you updated as to progress and also I will need to build a picture with you all about Owain and how his injuries affected his life.'

'They destroyed his life,' his mother spat. 'That John Berry and his wounds. He lost everything. Everything!' and she started to sob loudly.

Before Kim could move, Penny turned to her mother-in-law, putting her arm around her shoulder. 'It's alright, mother. Come on. At least something positive is being done. Owain didn't die in vain.'

'No, I suppose,' she sniffed. 'Still, it's so upsetting. That John Berry deserves to pay.'

'He already has, mother,' said Clive.

'Not good enough. No length of time would be good enough. When I think of what was taken from my boy!'

'I know,' Penny stroked the back of one of Kendra's hands.

'Will you be going back to Wales?' Kim asked Mrs Deans, in an effort to get her to think of something other than her loss.

'Not at the moment,' Clive answered for her. 'We think it's best she stays here for a while.' But his grimace said it all. Clive Deans wasn't enamoured of having his mother to stay.

'Clive and Penny are keen to look after me,' Kendra said with a dazzling smile.

Crane raised an eyebrow but kept quiet.

Once they had taken their leave, and were stood outside the house, Crane huffed out a breath. 'Thank goodness that's over,' he said.

'I think they took it rather well,' said Kim.

'I expect it's because they feel they'll get some sort of justice. Berry needs to pay for what he's done, that sort of thing.'

'More than the four years he's already served?' asked Kim.

'Judging by their reaction – yes.'

CHAPTER 20

'I need a room,' said Crane to Billy.

'A room? Isn't your desk good enough anymore?'

'What? Yes, yes, but I need a room to put in all the files that are going to be arriving.'

'Files?' Billy looked as though his head was elsewhere.

'The Owain Deans murder, Billy. Have you forgotten already?'

'Oh, right, yes, find one and leave me alone.' Billy looked down at the papers in his hand.

Crane hesitated, stumbled, unsure as to whether to go forwards or backwards.

'Well? Don't you understand? How about this - bugger off!'

'Fine. Okay. Sorry.' Crane backed out. Wondering when Billy had turned into Crane. Or at least the Crane he used to be. These days he didn't have any staff to be rude to.

'Dudley-Jones,' Crane called as he rapidly exited Billy's office. 'I need a room for the Owain murder case.'

'Take this one,' Dudley-Jones indicated his head left. 'The one on this side of my desk, it runs the length of the offices, if I remember rightly. I don't think anyone has ever used it.'

Crane walked over and opened a door he hadn't noticed before. The room did indeed run the length of the barracks and already had several trestle tables in it that he could use.

'Dudley-Jones, I could kiss you,' Crane said.

'Don't you bloody dare,' Dudley-Jones said and threw a ball of paper at his old boss.

Grinning, Crane hit the phones.

He firstly rang the police. 'Good morning,' he told the telephone operator. 'I'm trying to trace the paper files of an assault you prosecuted some five years ago.'

'Oh.'

'Is that it? Just Oh?' Crane was flustered. 'What on earth is the problem?'

'Five years ago, you said?'

'Yes. Five. Years.' He decided to speak as though the person on the phone didn't have English as their first language.

'It's just that we've changed our file management systems.'

'And that means what?'

'I'm not sure where your files are stored.'

'What are my files?'

'I beg your pardon?'

'You haven't asked me what case I'm looking for! Isn't that a bit odd? I'd say that was very relevant, wouldn't you?'

'Well, there's no need to be rude!'

'I wasn't trying to be rude.' Of course, Crane was. 'Let me put it another way. How do I get the files for case number A1543 John Berry assault on Owain Deans.'

'I don't know.'

Crane wanted to tear his hair out. 'Then who will?'

'I don't know.'

Now Crane wanted to tear his hair out by the roots. One strand at a time. 'Is there anyone else I can speak to?'

'Try the File Storage Department.'

'Good. Can you connect me?'

'No, they finish at 2pm on a Friday. Please call back on Monday.'

And the phone went dead. Not a good start. At this rate his lovely room was going to stay very empty.

'Dudley-Jones,' Crane called.

'Yes, Crane,' came the fed-up sounding reply.

'How do I find the files of John Berry assault on Owain Deans A1543.' Crane took a stab in the dark and used the CPS reference number.

Dudley-Jones clacked keys. 'That our case MPA 1511.'

'OK and where is that?'

'What?'

'The file!'

'On the One Drive system.'

'No, I mean the paper files.'

'On the One Drive system. There aren't any paper files. If you want paper files, you'll have to print them off.'

'From the One Drive system,' Crane said.

'You're catching on quick,' said Dudley-Jones, turning back to his computer screens.

Crane sighed. Grabbed his car keys. 'I'm going to think,' he said. 'I'll see you on Monday morning.'

'Say hi to Daniel for me,' Dudley-Jones called.

Crane raised his hand in the air in acknowledgement as he pushed his way out of the barracks. Collecting Daniel from school was mightily preferable to the problematic Deans case at that particular moment in time.

CHAPTER 21

Monday morning rolled around, as it always does, without fail, time and time again. It wasn't that Crane hated Monday mornings, indeed not, it was just sometimes that it was the routine of it all. He guessed it was because Daniel always moaned on a Monday about going back to school and yet by Monday afternoon, school was the coolest thing ever! Go figure.

And so, Crane came back to work rather more energised than he had been on Friday night. He popped into his room, to find piles of paper in it, that hadn't been there before.

'Dudley-Jones,' Crane called through the open door. 'What the hell is all this?'

His colleague appeared at the door. 'Oh, those. I printed the files off for you.'

'Bloody hell, thank you.'

'Well, I didn't want you getting in a mess with the printing and then getting all shouty at everyone.'

'Charming,' said Crane and turned on his heel, so Dudley-Jones wouldn't see the grin on his face. 'I suppose I best make you a coffee,' he called.

Coffee made, files printed off, it was now time to check in with the CPS. He was listening to the maddingly awful music on the phone, when it was eventually answered.

'Could I speak to the File Storage Department?'

'The what?' the operator sounded confused.

'The File Storage Department. I was told to ask for them.'

'Why?'

'Why what?'

'Why do you want them?'

'Jesus Christ,' Crane muttered. 'Because I want a file in storage.'

'But you have to put your request in writing.'

'Who to?'

'The File Storage Department. They only deal with email requests.'

'Thank you,' Crane said through gritted teeth. 'What's their email…' but the line was dead.

'For fuck's sake,' Crane threw his mobile across the table.

'Go online!' Dudley-Jones called.

'Online?'

'Yes, the CPS have a website and on there you will find the contact details for their departments.'

'You've done this before, haven't you?'

Dudley-Jones shrugged. 'You only had to ask,' he said with a sardonic grin, then ducked as the scrunched-up paper began to fly.

Crane wondered when he'd eventually get to do some detecting.

CHAPTER 22

'Thanks for seeing me, Mrs Deans,' Kim said.

She'd just arrived at Giles Dean's house, having arranged to see Owain's mother. She'd deliberately wanted to see her when both her son and her daughter-in-law were out at work.

They were sat in the lounge, with a tea tray between them. Kim poured them both a steaming cup.

'I'm glad to speak to you if it helps Owain, God rest his soul.' Mrs Deans crossed herself.

'Indeed,' said Kim, who despite being married to a Padre was still unsure as to her own faith and didn't wish to get drawn into a religious conversation. 'I just wanted to get a clearer idea of how on earth had Owain coped with his injuries?' she said. 'I did see him from time to time, but, of course, his family were closest to him.'

'He didn't. Cope that is. Sometimes he had coping strategies, but mostly he ignored them.'

'How do you mean?' Kim tucked her unruly hair behind one ear and leaned forward.

'Have you ever been rung in the middle of the night, by a drunk, crying into his cups?'

Kim smiled wryly, 'Yes, yes I have.'

'Well then, that's how it was with Owain. It had to get really bad before he called me. It really was the pits, his life, you know.'

'Yes, I do.'

'Then why are you asking me?'

'Because being his mother, you'd know more than anyone, what his mental state was like.'

'He was depressed, distraught, unable to cope with the physical part of his life. The tubes, the feeding, the stoma. He hated it all. He often said it would have been better if he'd had a leg blown off whilst at work. Then he would have had some respect, some money and support. As it was, he felt he had none of that.'

'He was invalided out of the army?'

'They couldn't wait to get rid of him. Wouldn't pay him a penny because the injury didn't happen at work and wouldn't give him his disability pension for the same reason. He felt let down and ignored.'

'I'm so sorry.'

'Oh, it wasn't your fault, girl. None of it was.'

'No, but maybe if I'd seen him more often…'

'It wouldn't have helped,' Mrs Deans reassured her. 'He was determined not to look after himself. I often think he wanted to die. The thing is, he ended up with a much different life than he would have had if he'd never been stabbed. That John Berry took my son's life from him. He may as well have killed him straight off. From the moment he was stabbed, Owain was just waiting to die.'

CHAPTER 23

Crane had had a generic email response to his request to the CPS for the John Berry case of assault on Owain Deans, but had heard nothing in several days. So, he once more hit the phone. To be told, 'You need to email the File Storage Department.'

'I've already done that. So please put me through.'

'Oh, very well.'

Despite the awful music, Crane had a smile on his face. Perhaps things would move along now.

'File Storage Department,' someone said in a sing song voice, worthy of a rendition of, 'Morning campers,' on Hi De Hi.

'Morning,' sang Crane back. 'I'm chasing up a file please.'

'Oh dear, you have to email in a request.'

'I've already done that.'

'Oh. For what file then?'

'A1543 please.'

'Oh.'

Crane was wondering if this person ever said anything other than the word oh. 'Oh, what? Where's my file?'

'Ah well, you see, there's a bit of a problem.'

'There is?' said Crane scratching at his beard in frustration at the slowness of the conversation.

'We've sort of lost it.'

'LOST IT?'

'Well, yes, but it's okay we've found it now.'

'Thank goodness for that.' Crane's heart rate slowed after such a shock.

'It's in Scotland.'

'What the blazes is it doing there?'

'There's no need to swear at me, Mr Crane.'

'Sgt Major Crane,' said Crane automatically.

'Yes, well, Sgt Major Crane your file is in Scotland. It will be here next week. Good day to you.'

Crane looked at the dead mobile, but didn't throw it this time, the poor thing was on its last legs. Between him throwing it and Daniel playing on it, it really was about time he bought a new one. Bloody Scotland. Jesus wept. He shook his head. You couldn't make this shit up! But he had to hang on, because of particular importance to Crane was the CPS court file including the summing up in the original trial and certificates of conviction for the original offence.

But life didn't get any better when he rang Aldershot police.

Crane revealed to the operator who he was, and that he wanted the file of the John Berry assault on Owain Deans.

'That could be awkward,' said the Desk Sergeant called Bevins, that Crane had been put through to, as the operator hadn't a clue.

Crane groaned.

'Well, it's just that it used to be in paper storage, but then we went digital.'

'Okay I can cope with that.'

'And now it's all on the cloud.'

Crane looked up but could only see blue sky without any clouds. 'The cloud?'

'Yes. Digital file storage and such. So, I can request it for you.'

'How?'

'I put a chitty in.'

Crane sighed. 'So let me get this right. It's all in the cloud. Digitized. But you put a piece of paper in requesting a digital file.'

'That's about the size of it.'

'Don't you think that's a bit mad?' Crane was shaking his head.

'It's not my job to think, Sgt Major. Just like the army, I'm paid to do as I'm told. It will be two weeks before the files arrive. You're not the only one who wants copies of files, you know, and we can't let all and sundry have access to our system.'

'Wait? What? Two weeks?'

But Crane was talking to himself. The chatty Sergeant was no doubt already talking to the next person in line.

It was a good job he had the Army files that Dudley-Jones had printed off for him. If he hadn't, he'd be way behind by now. As he trudged his way to his room, he wanted to look for the two witnesses that had called 999 that night.

He had to admit that one of the unforeseen challenges of the case was the recovery of the original assault case files. Due to the passage of time and changes in technology the recovery of the files was clearly proving problematic. Both the police and CPS had changed their file management systems, with the CPS having moved offices on a couple of occasions. The police had moved from a paper file system to one which was computer based.

Hang on a minute, thought Crane. Where was the paper file that the police used to create the digitized files. It must be somewhere. Surely it wouldn't have been destroyed. The thought made Crane shiver, then break out in a sweat.

He went back to the Desk Sergeant.

'Sgt Major Crane, here.'

'Oh, you again.'

'Yes, me again. If the files I want are now digitized,'

'Yes, I said that,' interrupted Sergeant Bevins.

'Then where are the paper files used to create the digitized files?'

'The paper files?'

'Yes. I want them requested from deep storage and they should contain the original statements, unused material and original exhibits. Shouldn't they?'

'Well, yes, I suppose so.'

'So can I request them please?'

'From me?'

'From whoever has them.'

'That will be deep storage.'

'Well, get them from them. Thank you.'

And that time Crane had the last word.

CHAPTER 24

'He just couldn't cope, you know,' said Giles as he showed Kim into the lounge of their house in Frimley. 'Owain. It was all very depressing.'

Kim was interviewing Owain's brother, Giles and his wife Penny. She hadn't managed to split them up, unfortunately.

'He had this attitude, though, didn't he?' said Penny.

'What do you mean?' Giles rounded on her.

'Well, it was always poor me, wasn't it? Never, I won't be defined by my life changing injuries.'

'Oh.'

It seemed Giles didn't have any other retort to that, so Kim took the statement as the truth. 'It takes a special kind of person to be able to do that,' she said.

'Yes, I suppose so,' mumbled Penny. 'We did all try and support him.'

'I'm sure you did,' agreed Kim.

'It was just that he couldn't cope,' said Giles.

'With his injuries?'

'Yes, those and no longer being in the army. There he was told what to do, when and how to do it. Then he was suddenly on his own, with no support or back up from his lads. I mean what the hell does a marine do, when he can't be a marine?'

And that was the crux of it, thought Kim. As his mother had said, Berry, to all intents and purposes, had killed Owain when he plunged the knife into his stomach. It just took five years for him to die.

'We were always calling the doctor for him, weren't we?' Giles said to Penny.

'Oh, God, yes. I'd forgotten.'

'The doctor? You mean his GP?'

Giles nodded. 'He was forever doing stuff to himself.'

'And not doing stuff he was supposed to,' said Penny.

'Like?'

'Like refusing entry to medical staff who called at his home, and he refused to have blood tests a couple of times.'

'That's right,' agreed Gavin. 'And he refused to cooperate with mental health assessments as well.'

'I suspect there are more things,' said Penny. 'I don't think he managed his Hickman line very well.'

'Thanks for that,' said Kim making a note. 'You've both been very helpful thank you so much and if you think of anything else, perhaps you'd call me?' She held out a card, which Penny took.

'Of course, we will,' she said and deliberately looked at her husband. 'Won't we?'

'Yes, dear.'

Kim supressed a smile and took her leave.

She sat in her car for a few minutes, thinking about Owain Deans. He certainly had come over as a tortured soul on the few times she'd met him. But she'd never taken him for a stupid man. So why hadn't he followed the medical advice? Because that's certainly what it sounded like. Had he really not followed it, because he didn't want to live like that? Or had he not followed it because he wanted some attention from his family? Either way, Crane needed to know about Owain's behaviour. He needed to know how bad it actually was.

CHAPTER 25

Crane was just leaving for the night when the phone on his desk rang. Frowning he realised that he couldn't ignore it. Never had been able to. So, he picked it up.

'Sgt Major Crane.'

'Ah, glad I've caught you. It's Bevins the Desk Sergeant at Aldershot Police Station.'

'Hello. What can I do for you?'

'It's more what I can do for you. Or rather, not do for you, I suppose.'

'Stop talking in riddles, man and get on with it. I'd like to see my son before he goes to sleep tonight.'

Crane could hear a deep breath from the other man. 'It's the files from deep storage.'

'Oh great, you have them, then.'

'Not exactly.'

'Tell me what the problem is, then. There is obviously a problem.'

'During the original assault John Berry used a knife. This was shown during the original assault trial, and, after conviction, a destruction order was issued.'

'Destruction,' Crane said weakly.

'Yes. So now Owain Dean's death is being investigated and we want the original weapons, I've found the knife had been destroyed.'

'You just said that. Is there more?'

'I'm afraid so. No photographs had been taken of the weapon and there is no description of it.'

'Mmm,' Crane said shrugging off his coat and sitting down.

'I guess we can live without the knife or the pictures, as it has already been established that the original assault is not in question, the presence of weapons at trial will become less important.'

'Another key piece of evidence is the 999-call made by the two witnesses, to the ambulance service. The police no longer have possession of a copy of the call. It seems that the Ambulance Service have changed their recording methods, and it will take some time to recover the call from archives.'

'That's supposing they can find it.'

'Yes,' said Sgt Bevins, candidly.

'Have you become my unofficial contact at Aldershot Police?' Crane mused aloud.

'It would seem so, Sir.'

'Alright then, Bevins, I look forward to you finding the copy of the call at least, as you can't really produce anything else.' And with that Crane slammed down the phone. He always found that far more satisfying than just pressing the mobile phone screen.

CHAPTER 26

If Crane couldn't get a copy of the call, then he needed to find the witnesses and confirm their statements. He also needed them to be able to attend as witnesses should the case eventually get to court.

Jeremy Cheshire was easy enough to track down. He was still in the same house as he'd been in five years ago, which was just around the corner from Owain Deans. More than that, his girlfriend Diane was now his wife and so the couple were still together. Crane thanked Dudley Jones profusely and called Jeremy, whom he arranged to meet after work.

After letting Crane in, Jeremy explained, 'This was my mother's house and when she passed three years ago now, I stayed here and her life insurance cleared the mortgage.'

'That was when he proposed,' said Diane beaming. 'We've been married two years now,' she said.

'Congratulations,' said Crane who felt he had to say something about it. 'Now, about Owain Deans,' turning to what was far more important as far as Crane was concerned.

'Dreadful business,' said Jeremy.

'I can't talk about this without a coffee,' Diane said leaping up from the settee where she sat next to her husband and scuttled off to the kitchen.

'Is Mrs Cheshire alright?' Crane asked.

'Yes, fine, the truth is she gets embarrassed.'

'Embarrassed? About what?'

'About what was happening in John Berry's house.'

'You mean Owain Dean's house.'

'Yes, exactly. But we didn't know about Owain at all. He was never there when John had one of his parties. And we never went round when he was, so as far as we were concerned, it was John's house.'

Crane nodded, 'I see. I can understand that.'

'Well, that morning was a case of the morning after the night before.'

'Here we are,' said Diane, enthusiastically carrying a tray into the room. 'Now, Mr Crane, do you have milk and sugar?'

'No, thanks, I'll take it black. What happened when Owain came home then?' he urged Jeremy.

'We were upstairs in what we thought was the spare room.

'Yes.'

'But it wasn't. It turned out to be Owain's room,' Diane joined in. 'It was so embarrassing. We were in his bed. He, Owain, threw our clothes out of the bedroom and we had to scuttle after them.'

'That means you were downstairs when it happened.'

'The stabbing, you mean?'

'Yes, the stabbing.'

'We were downstairs dressing, when we saw John brandishing a knife and running up the stairs.'

'He was calling for Owain,' said Diane, 'who came out of his bedroom.'

'Then John ran up the stairs at him, holding out the knife,' said Jeremy.

'And Owain ran down. I don't think he saw the knife,' said Diane.

'He mustn't have done, he wouldn't have run down otherwise,' Jeremy explained.

'No, I guess not,' said Diane. 'Anyway, as I was saying, he ran onto the knife.'

'No, that's not quite right. John moved his arms and stabbed Owain. Owain didn't stumble, didn't fall on them, didn't deliberately stab himself,' insisted Jeremy.

No, sorry you're right,' said Diane. 'John ran up the stairs and deliberately stabbed Owain.'

'Repeatedly,' said Jeremy.

'If needed to, would you be willing to give a formal statement?' asked Crane.

'Why yes, of course, but why?' Jeremy looked confused.

'Because Owain is dead, and John Berry is accused of his murder.' Crane saw no need to sugar coat what had happened.

'Oh God,' Diane's hand flew to her mouth.

'Bloody hell.' Jeremy looked physically shaken.

'Are you still in touch with John?' Crane wanted to know.

Jeremy shook his head. 'No not much since the stabbing. Of course, he went off to prison, so it wasn't like we saw him at the corner shop.'

'I also understand you rang 999. Which one of you did that?'

'I shouted we needed to call 999,' Diane answered Crane.

'And I did it,' said Jeremy.

'Can you remember what you said?'

'Just that someone had been stabbed. There was a lot of blood and Owain had just lost consciousness.'

'What did John do?'

'Just stood there,' explained Jeremy.

'He dropped the knife,' remembered Diane.

'Oh yes, so he did.'

'He was arrested as soon as the police arrived.'

'Had you asked for the police?' said Crane.

'No, the emergency operator said she'd told them and that the police would be with us in a few minutes,' said Jeremy.

'So, the authorities took care of everything.'

'Oh yes, they took us into the living room. I heard them arresting John.'

'And the ambulance paramedics were working on Owain. They sent for the air ambulance and within, what, 15 minutes he was gone on his way to hospital,' explained Diane.

'That was the last time we saw either of them,' finished Jeremy.

Crane couldn't thank them enough for their detailed recall and also for their willingness to help.

'To be honest, Sgt Major, it has never left us. I can still see the events of that day clearly in my mind.'

'While I have nightmares about it,' shuddered Diane.

Crane knew all about that.

CHAPTER 27

The one thing Crane was actually looking forward to, was talking to Anderson about the case. He'd wanted to see Derek and Jean since Derek retired, but they'd been on an extended holiday – a cruise no less. It seemed Jean had been saving up for years, for the event of Anderson's retirement, when Anderson would finally have time for her and for their family.

When Crane met Anderson at a local pub, he did a quick double take. Gone was the wispy grey hair across the top of his head. It had been trimmed back to where he was going bald. Gone was the pallid skin from working indoors too much, he now had a healthy glowing tan. Gone was the tiredness that used to dog each step, he now sprang into the pub. As he drew nearer, Crane could see Anderson had dropped a few pounds as well. It made Crane feel exhausted just looking at him.

'Bloody hell,' burst from his lips before he could stop it.

Anderson laughed. 'Hello to you too, Crane.'

'I'm sorry, but have you seen my friend Derek Anderson anywhere? I'm meeting him here for a drink.'

'Ha bloody ha,' said Anderson. 'By the way, thanks for the pint,' and he toasted Crane with it.

'Seriously, mate, you look amazing. You've lost at least 5 years.'

'Jean reckons 10, but I'll take 5. I never knew how ill I actually was until I left the job. Gradually layer after layer of work, bad food, exhaustion, pressure, fell away. It's like I'd forgotten who I was.'

'You're still a copper at heart thought, aren't you?' It would shake Crane's world if someone like Anderson could slough off the job that had defined him for 30 years.

'Too right, but don't tell the wife.'

Crane's world settled back on its access, and he felt able to tell Anderson one of the reasons he'd wanted to get together.

'Apart from my sparkling personality,' grinned Anderson.

'Aye, apart from that,' and Crane quickly put Anderson in the picture.

'God, I remember that poor bloke,' said Anderson. 'The case was before we started working together. Never seen anything like it, his stomach that is. He was so very ill, I'm surprised he didn't pass away.'

'Well, he has now,' said Crane and explained the circumstances.

'Wow. Murdered five years after the event.'

'That's what they reckon. I'm just in the process of collating all the background information from the case and the court process.'

'So, what do you want from me?'

'I want to interview you. Get your thoughts and recollections of Owain Deans. What do you reckon?'

'Recorded?'

'Yes, a proper interview.'

There was silence.

'Please?' urged Crane.

'What?' Anderson seemed to shake himself. 'Sorry I was just thinking about Owain. Yes, yes, of course I'll help.'

CHAPTER 28

Crane needed to get hold of Owain Dean's medical records, one from Aldershot Health Centre, one from the Army and one from the hospital. But no one would talk to him. No one would give him anything. They wanted proof. A death certificate and Crane's identification. His military police identification wasn't any good as it didn't say he was a soldier, and it only showed his name and his photo. Plus, the civilian authorities would only release records by request of the police.

Anderson was out of the police now, so he couldn't help. Which meant that Crane had to go to Bevins.

He called him at the station. 'Ah, Sgt Bevins, Crane here from Provost Barracks. Would you do me a favour?'

'Really? Me do you a favour?'

'Yes, please, Bevins, I need copies of medical records.'

'And you need me to request them.'

'Absolutely. Spot on.'

'Oh, very well, send me the details and I'll get round to it.'

'This morning. You'll get round to it this morning. Because, as you know, we'll have to wait a while for them to come in. So, the sooner the better. Please.' Crane was really grovelling now.

'Fucking hell, alright, Crane.'

Crane wanted to remind him that he was Sgt Major Crane but thought that would probably be a bad idea at that particular moment. Instead, he took himself off to Frimley Park hospital and in particular to the morgue.

***

He found Major Martin in his office and knocked politely.

Martin looked up. 'Oh! Crane, you gave me a fright.'

'Sorry, sir. I wondered if I might have a word?'

'Feel free, here sit down, it's a quiet day, so far at least. Now what can I do for you?'

Crane filled the Major in on what had been happening since the autopsy he did on Owain Deans.

Major Martin nodded. 'I remember that well. Poor sod, his stomach wasn't half a mess.'

'Indeed. But the thing is I need your report on the autopsy and more importantly where you talk about the causal link between the original stabbing and the death of Owain Deans.'

'That's easy enough,' said the Major and moved to open a filing cabinet. 'Here's what I submitted to the Coroner,' he said and handed Crane a file.

After skimming it and confirming it was the original that Crane had a copy of, he said, 'For the case to succeed we need a strong causal link between the original stabbing and Owain's death. You have stated that, based on the information available, there was strong clinical and pathological evidence that the abdominal injuries sustained by Owain, had made a significant contribution to his death.'

'Exactly,' agreed Major Martin. 'To me it's as plain as the nose on my face.'

'But what about his medical history?' Crane said. 'I know I haven't got it all, but from what I can gather his medical history following the stabbing has been long and complicated. The original injury was a potentially fatal penetrating to his abdomen requiring life-saving emergency surgery. He suffered intestinal failure, meaning he was unable to adequately absorb food.'

'That's correct,' said Major Martin. 'Had he not been given TPN directly into his bloodstream he would have starved to death.'

Crane shuddered.

'In my view,' Major Martin continued, 'there is no doubt that alcohol abuse and failure to comply with medical advice contributed to his terminal decline. Nevertheless, it is also quite clear that he would not have had to cope with the Hickman line, TPN and his trauma if he had not been stabbed by Berry.'

'And will you put that in writing?'

'Of course, Crane, I'll amend the autopsy report to add my additional thoughts and findings and send you through a copy.'

That was music to Crane's ears. He could only hope that it was enough to persuade the CPS that John Berry should be charged with murder.

CHAPTER 29

'Thank you for coming in, Detective Inspector Anderson,' said Crane formally as Derek appeared at Provost Barracks.

'Retired,' Anderson said with a wink.

Crane grinned. 'Excuse me, retired.' Then Crane was all formality, as he'd earlier explained to Anderson. He made sure the tape and the video link were working, then said, 'I've asked you here today to take your statement regarding your involvement with the Owain Deans case. Unfortunately, as sometimes happens your original statement has been lost, which is why we're taking it again.'

'No problem, I'm glad to help.'

'Thank you. I also see you've brought your notebook with you?'

'Yes, I thought that might help with my recollections and, of course, you can use it when you're collating all the paperwork for the CPS.'

'Thank you, again. Now when did you first hear of this case?'

'I was the senior investigating officer on duty the night the 999-call came in, so I was one of the first officers to arrive and from then on it was my case.'

What followed was a remarkable recall into the ins and outs of the case and Crane was extremely grateful to his friend for his attention to detail.

'Oh, and by the way,' Anderson finished, fishing something out of his pocket. 'I'd kept a copy of the audio tape of the interviews I conducted with John Berry, so I've done you a copy. Just to use until you get the originals that is,' said Derek.

'Actually, that might be more valuable than you might think,' said Crane. 'All the files, interviews and 999 tapes seem to have gone walk about. I've got Sgt Bevins trying to locate all the missing items, but to be honest we don't hold out much hope. The knife, of course, had been destroyed.'

'Really? But it's an exhibit in an attempted murder trial!' Anderson was incensed.

'You didn't know then? I didn't think you did. Well how about this one, did you know there's not so much as a photograph of the weapon.'

'Bloody hell!'

'Exactly,' agreed Crane. 'It's a good job the bastard pled guilty to GBH, otherwise I'd be up shit creek without a paddle.'

CHAPTER 30

Crane looked around his incident room. Finally, it was full of files with his tables groaning under the weight of them. What did it all mean though? The police, the doctors and the CPS had done a thorough job, getting ready for a trial that never was, to prove that John Berry had stabbed his so-called friend repeatedly in the stomach five years ago. There was some merit in the call that Berry had been under the influence of drugs at the time, which accounted for the change in his personality, but the police had never had any truck with that excuse.

Berry had pled guilty. Which meant all the files hadn't necessarily been kept as there hadn't been a full trial. He'd pled guilty. Got sentenced. Served his sentence. Then pissed off.

Would they be able to find him again? If they could, for any case against Berry to be successful, the prosecution would need to show a causal link between the act or omission and the cause of death. In this case the act was the stabbing of Owain by John. His act was not the sole cause of death but must have contributed significantly to Owain's death. That had been covered by Major Martin.

The medical records had finally come through, thanks to Sgt Bevins and a review of them showed a documented history of alcohol abuse and non-compliance with medical treatment and advice. Also, Owain had a history of repeated infections in his abdomen and latterly in his Hickman line. Kim had been right to give him the heads up about that. As a result, Crane had been able to explore that with Major Martin, who was still very much of the opinion that there was a strong causal link between the stabbing and Owain's death some five years later.

Major Martin concluded that the stab wound was a major underlying cause of his death and that the cause of death of Owain Deans was septicaemia due to intestinal failure and infarction due to complications of penetrating abdominal injury and surgery.

Crane had managed to tick everything off on his list and the paperwork was now ready to be submitted to the CPS via DI Lawrence Wood of Aldershot Police.

But there was still one problem.

They couldn't find John Berry.

CHAPTER 31

Crane walked out of the incident room and loitered by Dudley-Jones.

'Yes, Crane, what do you want?' Jones asked without taking his eyes from his computer screen.

'Where the hell is John Berry? I've just been over the files. We now have everything we need. Except the perpetrator.'

'Ah, well, it's just that...'

'Just that what?'

'Probation service have lost him!'

'For fuck's sake! I thought they were supposed to know where he was. He was out on licence, wasn't he?'

'Yes,' agreed Dudley-Jones

'Which meant he could be recalled to prison for any misdemeanour, never mind something huge like this!'

'Yep, you could put it like that, Crane.'

'Jesus, well give me his last known address.'

Crane's phone pinged. 'Who the hell is that?' he chunnered.

'It's me, Crane, I've sent you a text with the last known address for John Berry.'

'God save me from technology. What on earth was wrong with you telling me?'

Crane stomped out of the office, looking at his phone. The address was a hostel in Winchester. A kind of halfway house, Crane supposed. Oh well, he best go and see if anyone would talk to him there.

As Crane sat in his car, he punched in Winchester into the sat nav. There it was. About 50 minutes journey. Either the A31 or the M3. Crane reasoned the M3 would feel faster being motorway and opted for that.

Infact the M3 proved to be as boring as hell. He decided he'd go back via the A31, to keep him awake more than anything. Parking near the hostel, he walked around the corner and took a minute or two to look at the premises. It seemed pretty nondescript, looking like any other building in the street, which seemed to be mostly commercial premises. There was no big signage exclaiming what the building was, which Crane kind of got. There was no one going in or out. Infact, no activity of any sort. He sauntered over to the front door, where there was a sign that said everyone had to be out by 10 am and would not be able to return until 5pm. That explained the lack of activity. Underneath the sign was a bell. So he rang it.

'No entry until 5pm,' a disembodied voice said through a speaker.

'I wonder if I can see the manager?'

'No entry until 5pm,' the voice said again.

'For God's sake, man,' said Crane. 'I'm with the military police, investigating a murder, now can I come in and see the manager?'

After a short moment of silence, the door creaked open. In front of him stood an overweight man, wearing a stained white shirt that stretched over his belly, causing the buttons to strain and holes to form in between them.

'What do you want?' the man drawled, as though he were a two-bit criminal from a movie.

Crane walked in and physically pushed the man aside.

'Oy,' he yelled.

But Crane ignored him and grabbed the signing in book.

'When did you last see John Berry?' he asked, flicking through the pages. 'He came to you when he was let out of prison some three months ago now. It seems he's absconded, and the Probation Service can't find him.'

'Not my problem,' growled the man.

Crane took in the filthy man, the filthy carpet and the nothing short of disgusting mess in the office that Crane could see through the hatch, on which rested the signing in book. A sign above the hatch said, 'Dave Finch – Manager.

'Look,' Crane said. 'I can see you don't give a shit, probably don't get paid enough money to care, but can you please at least try and help me to find John Berry.'

Finch looked at Crane for a moment, then walked around him to the office door. Getting a key from a chain on his belt, Finch opened the door to the office.

Crane had no wish to follow him and remained where he was. Finch opened a file drawer and after flicking through the files, drew one out.

'Here you are,' he said holding it out. 'John's file. You can keep it. I don't need it anymore.'

'Thank you,' said Crane and let himself out.

Glad to be out in the fresh air, he walked around to his car. Resisting the urge to read the file in the car, he turned his vehicle around and drove back to Aldershot, still feeling as though the filth and squalor of the halfway house was clinging to his suit.

**

That night Crane read the file after Daniel was asleep. It was brief and to the point. John had moved into the facility upon being released from jail. In the time he was there, three weeks, he didn't have a job, didn't seem to make any friends, was reluctant to help with the basic chores and it seemed he couldn't wait to get out of there. Finch assumed that John had found alternative accommodation when he didn't return after three days. End of file. End of responsibility.

Crane's sleep, later, was interrupted by the most awful nightmare. It was Owain Deans. He was lying on the slab in the mortuary, start bollock naked with all his abdominal injuries on display and signs that the sepsis had spread throughout his stomach, as it was mottled black and blue, as though he'd been punched. But it was the blood and infection that had seeped out of his intestines. Major Martin was conducting the autopsy. As Crane watched Major Martin open up Owain with a Y incision, the poor man turned his head, opened his eyes, looked straight and Crane and said, 'Please help me.'

Crane woke in a sweat and a tangle of duvet, his heart going nineteen to the dozen. Reaching for the water on his bedside cabinet, he gulped it down, then collapsed back on his pillows, doubting he'd get any more sleep that night.

He had to find John Berry. So, the next morning Crane rang Diane Chambers, the Editor of the Aldershot News.

ALDERSHOT NEWS

Here at the Aldershot News we are glad to assist the Military Police and the Aldershot Police in their quest to find a man called John Berry, aka The Weasel. This was the nick name he was known by, when he served four years in Winchester Prison.

He was there due to being found guilty of Grievous Bodily Harm with a knife, upon a poor man called Owain Deans, who had done nothing more than a good turn, sharing his home with a fellow human being, at reasonable rent. Deans was a Marine, based at Aldershot Garrison, fit, healthy and loving life. After the knife attack, he was left in excruciating pain, unable to eat, fed through a tube and with a colostomy bag. His career in the British Army over. His life left in tatters.

Poor Owain Deans has since died from his injuries and there is now a warrant out for the arrest of John Berry. This picture shows him upon entry to Winchester Prison some four years ago. However, known associates have said that he doesn't look much different, it's just that his hair is shorter.

If you do see him, the police urge that you please do not approach him but dial 999 immediately.

CHAPTER 32

Early consultation with local CPS lawyers had proved useful in explaining the complicated details of the case and to express the police's commitment to investigate and progress it. Crane, of course, had been present at that meeting. Once all the paperwork was ready, he and the Aldershot Police submitted everything they had. Then held their collective breaths.

The following month, the decision was made.

'Crane!' called Dudley-Jones. 'There's an email on the system for you from the CPS regarding the Owain Deans case!'

'Oh God,' said Crane, torn between wanting the verdict if it was good news and not wanting it if it was bad. He felt like a kid getting the envelope with his exam results in. 'Have you read it?'

'No, of course not, it's for you!'

'Read it. I can't.'

'Oh, very well.'

The silence was deafening. 'Well?' asked Crane walking to Dudley-Jones' desk thinking that actually it was worse than getting exam results.

'Shit!' exclaimed Dudley-Jones.

Crane deflated. 'That bad?'

'Yes, the CPS have decided that there is insufficient evidence to establish a causal link between the original assault and the death five years later and they have decided to take no further action.'

'What the fuck!'

'I know, that really stinks, Crane.'

Crane prowled the office. 'I'm not having it. I mean it! I'm not going to let this rest!'

Crane's mobile rang, interrupting his diatribe. It was DI

Lawrence Wood from Aldershot Police.

'Have you read the email?' he said.

'Yes,' snapped Crane. He'd never liked the man and still didn't. But he was police and Crane wasn't anything much, so he had to work with him. Aldershot police were his route to getting convictions. And he needed them onside.

'We don't agree with this decision,' said Lawrence. 'And will make further representations to the lawyer concerned and the Head of the Branch.'

'Will that help?' said Crane, who was rapidly descending into a pit of anger and despair. He couldn't let this happen to Owain Deans. No further action. How dare they! That wasn't justice. That wasn't fair.

'Who knows,' came the reply. 'But we have to try.'

For once Crane agreed with DI Wood, but he didn't hold out much hope. Crane prowled the office until Dudley Jones told him to fuck off. So he did. He walked.

Going along Queens Avenue in the blustery wind, Crane remembered the times he'd taken a walk to cool off, or to try and unknot a sticky problem. He'd often met Padre Symmonds if he'd got the timing right. Crossing the road to the large expanse of grass, he raised his head and would you believe it, there was Padre Symmonds. Crane hurried to meet him.

'Well, I never,' said the Padre, shaking Crane's hand. 'I hadn't banked on seeing you today!'

'Me neither, Padre,' said Crane. 'But I'm glad I have.'

The Padre must have noticed the growl in Crane's voice. 'Come on, spill it, what's wrong?'

And that was all the encouragement Crane needed, telling the Padre of the decision by the CPS to take no further action in the Deans case. 'Can you believe it? The bastards! Turning me down. How dare they!' he roared.

'Hum, it's clear you're mad, but who at exactly?' said Padre Symmonds.

'Sorry?' Crane stopped walking.

'Who are you mad with? Yourself? Owain Deans? John Berry?

The CPS?'

Crane's mouth dropped open.

'Okay, let's break it down. You're mad with yourself for failing to persuade the CPS to prosecute. You're mad with Owain Deans for not dealing with his injuries like a man. With John Berry for stabbing Owain in the first place. Oh, and the CPS for being spineless idiots.'

Crane's mouth was still open, so he put his head back and roared his anger to the skies.

Then he took a deep breath and said, 'You're right, of course.' Crane couldn't stop his fists clenching. 'But, but, I just feel so impotent. I'm working and working but in the end I'm not making a difference. And it makes me so angry.'

'Then get even.'

'Sorry?'

The Padre said, 'Get even, not angry. Or is it the other way around. Don't get angry, get even. Anyway, which ever it is, you need to get rid of that anger and then do something with it. Channel that anger into making sure you get justice for Owain. For that's what all this is for, isn't it?'

Crane nodded. 'Thank you, Padre,' he said and walked away. Back to Provost Barracks. Back to making John Berry pay.

Crane got the call later that day.

'Any news?' snapped Crane. He couldn't seem to help himself.

'Unsuccessful I'm afraid,' said Lawrence Wood.

'Bollocks. Surely there's something else we can do. Owain was a fellow soldier. I can't leave it like this.' Crane was drained. Beyond anger. He knew that it wouldn't achieve anything, and he had to persuade the police to up the anti. He needed to be nice.

'The only thing left is an appeal to the head of the CPS. My Superintendent is arranging that now. But there might be yet another delay while we wait for a decision, and we can't guarantee the outcome.' Lawrence sounded as crushed as Crane felt.

'I understand,' said Crane. 'Look, thanks for all your help.'

'You did the work, Crane. The thanks is all yours.'

'But I can't submit anything, and you lot can. It's just... just...'

Crane swallowed a lump in his throat. 'I do appreciate all your help.' Crane closed the call before he lost it completely.

He'd never wanted a cigarette more in his life, so he wandered outside. But of course, he wouldn't smoke one, didn't even have one, had given up a long time ago.

But it just showed the hold nicotine could have on a body.

CHAPTER 33

Every day Crane rang to speak to DI Wood about the case. Every time he got the message that DI Wood would be in touch. Then Crane had taken to stalking him at the police station, but that didn't bring results either. It seemed that Wood was determined to keep Crane in his place and only contact Crane when he had something to say. This was playing out the same as Crane's case earlier in the year.

Crane called into the police station and chatted to Sgt Bevins but got nowhere there either. 'Come on, Crane,' he'd said. 'I know you had a position within Aldershot Police curtesy of DI Anderson. But all that's changed now. A new broom has swept through CID. He who shall be obeyed, has spoken.'

He'd said that earlier in the year, as well. It just showed nothing changed.

Finally, there was a text. From DI Woods. Crane took a deep breath and opened the message. The relief was such that he nearly cried. He realised how much the case meant to him. How big a hold it had on him. He'd always tried to not get emotionally involved, but sometimes it was hard not to. The way Owain had been injured. The pain and suffering he'd endured. The loss of his life, his livelihood, all that he held dear.

Finally, the appeal had been successful.

Now where the hell was John Berry?

***

Kim Symmonds was out and about in Aldershot and realised that she was near Owain Dean's house. She turned a corner and there it was. The house had been sold after Owain's death and no doubt the new owners had settled in and knew nothing of the previous occupant, other than he was deceased. She was just about to drive off, when a woman came out of the house next door. Seeing Kim, she waived, and Kim got out of her car.

'Hi,' Kim said. 'How are you?'

'Oh, you know. Getting by, just like everyone else. I meant to say to you what a lovely service your hubby did for dear Owain.'

Kym suppressed a smile. It was strange to hear Padre Symmonds called 'your hubby' and would no doubt give Francis a laugh. But to hear her call Owain 'dear' was just as awkward. The names she used to call Owain when he was disturbing the peace, after drinking too much, not feeding himself and generally getting in a fog. He had been known to throw cans and bottles into the street and shout John Berry's name over and over, threatening to kill the bastard.

'Such a shame what happened to him. It's all that bloke's fault really, that Berry.'

Kim nodded her agreement then went to get back into her car. But the neighbour wasn't finished.

'Saw him the other day. That Berry. The weasel. I meant to ring the police, like the paper said, but forgot by the time I got home. I don't have a mobile so I couldn't do it straight away.'

Kim stilled. 'You saw him?'

'Yes, down by the church, think he was going to the food bank. I didn't speak to him. Scares me he does. Someone who could try and kill a bloke. No, I kept out of his way I can tell you.'

'Which Church?' said Kim leaning on the car door, knowing full well that John Berry hadn't been seen in the Garrison Church.

'The Baptist Church. Down near the town.'

'And what day was that did you say?'

'Couple of days ago, um, yes, Monday it was as I was on my way to the post office.'

Kim thanked the woman and saying that she must get on, she climbed into her car and drove. Using her hands-free system, she called Crane.

'John Berry is back in the area,' she told him.

'What? Really?'

'Yes, he mustn't know Owain is dead, otherwise he'd never show his face here.'

'He's supposed to be in Winchester.'

'Well, he was seen on Monday by Owain's neighbour near the Baptist Church. Apparently, they have a good food bank there.'

'Is she sure?'

'She is, after all she lived next door to him.'

'Well done, Kim,' he said.

'I didn't do anything, just happened to be in the right place at the right time.'

'Well thanks anyway, I owe you one.'

And then he was gone.

CHAPTER 34

Crane was anxious to trace John Berry and he was indebted to Kim for the information she'd picked up. After that conversation, Crane got in his car and went to the food bank.

There was a queue outside and inside he could see volunteers in tabards filling plastic bags with tins and packets. He knocked on the door, despite the cat calls from the queue.

'Where the hell do you think you're going?'

'There's a queue here, idiot!'

'We're all fucking hungry mate so get to the back.'

Crane smiled in a sort of apology and held his ID up to the door hoping held be let in. At last, someone came and opened the door.

'Yes? Can I help you?' the woman seemed all hard angles as though she didn't have enough to eat herself. Crane saw thin arms with knobbly elbows, legs with matching knobbly knees. Her hair brittle and blond. 'I've got lots of hungry clients to feed so get on with it.'

After introducing himself he asked for her name.

'Angie Battle. I'm the manager.'

Crane held up a photo of John Berry. 'I understand this man has been seen at your food bank.'

She squinted at the photo. 'So what?'

'So, I'm trying to find him.'

'Why?'

Crane decided to go all in, he didn't think she'd help otherwise. 'He's wanted for murder.'

'Oh!' her hand went to her mouth. 'What on earth…'

Crane gave her a card. 'If you see him, please could you give me a ring.'

She nodded mutely.

'It seems he's either on the run or lying low somewhere. Just act normal if you see him. But text me right away. Would that be ok?'

She nodded again.

'Thank you. I'll leave you to get on.'

Crane turned on his heel, opened the door and made a quick exit.

***

It was two days later that Crane got a text. 'He is here now,' it said.' Come quickly.'

Crane ran for his car, or at least ran the best he could. Swinging into the traffic on Queens Avenue, willy nilly, he drove off to a cacophony of car horns. But Crane didn't care. He was desperate to get to the Baptist Church.

Just as he pulled up, he saw the weasel grabbing for a bus and swinging himself onboard.

'Got you,' said Crane and he sat patiently in his car behind the bus, despite some motorists thinking he should be overtaking the thing. Well, he would have done if he hadn't been following a man.

The bus trundled away, and Crane trundled behind it. He had to admit it must be the slowest form of transport around. Using his hands-free phone system, he rang Dudley-Jones.

'Where does the number 18 bus go?'

'Um, hang on, just getting it, here we are, Bordon and Whitehill are the ultimate destinations.'

'Great, thanks.'

'Is that where you are then?'

'I'm following a bus with John Berry on it.'

'Bloody hell, well done.'

'Well, I've got to get hold of him first. Jesus Christ the bloody bus is stopping again!' And with that Crane cancelled the call.

He followed it as it arrived in Bordon. That's good, thought Crane, lots of open spaces and the houses on the barracks are quite spaced out. I should be able to get to him easily.

But that wasn't the case. Well, it never was, was it, thought Crane as he saw John Berry get off the bus. Hurrying to park his car by the small parade of shops, he saw Berry taking off down an alleyway. As soon as he turned the engine off, Crane struggled out of the car, and went into the alleyway that John had taken.

The trouble was, the road entered a maze of an estate and, of course, Crane's leg wasn't up to much, as Berry nipped along the streets. Then the inevitable happened. Crane lost him.

'Shit, fuck, bollocks,' he said. He rang Dudley-Jones, 'I've lost the bastard. Couldn't keep up with this gammy leg.'

'Don't worry I'll put out a wanted man request to the police. Ask them to do more patrols, even door to door if they've the manpower.'

'Thanks,' said Crane. 'I'm coming back to the office. If I can ever find my bastard car!'

CHAPTER 35

It's strange how sometimes the planets align. After his nonsense running after John Berry, Crane had to go and see the physio at Frimley Park. Afterwards navigating the many corridors and lifts, Crane was walking through a ward and there he was. John Berry.

Crane grabbed a nurse, flashed his ID and asked, 'What is the matter with John Berry?'

'He was diagnosed with possible kidney failure and is currently having tests, which is the reason for him sitting in a huge chair with a canula in one hand, with a drip attached,' she said.

The nurse went on about Berry's debilitating problem, but Crane wasn't having any of it.

'The bloke ran quite spritely two days ago, when I was trying to arrest him.'

'But he's not supposed to do that!' exclaimed the nurse. 'He's to keep quiet, keep exercise to a minimum and be careful what he eats and drinks.'

'You should tell him that, not me,' said Crane grinning.

Pulling out his mobile phone he talked to Aldershot police and asked that someone come and arrest John Berry for skipping off when he was on licence.

'How long will he be here?' he asked the nurse.

'Another couple of hours, I suppose.'

'That'll do nicely,' said Crane. 'I'll go and grab and coffee and be back by the time the police arrive to arrest him.'

'How can you do that? He's a sick man!'

'So was the bloke who Berry stabbed and is now dead. So, weasel over there might be ill, but his victim is dead.'

Within the hour, DI Wood met Crane at Frimley Park Hospital. Crane had rung the police and informed Sgt Bevins that Crane knew where Berry was, who must have alerted the DI.

'Good work, Crane,' Wood said as he appeared next to Crane, who was ostensibly waiting to be treated in the area opposite Berry. As Berry had no idea who Crane was, or what he looked like, he would have no idea that he was under observation. Therefore, he was still sat there, eyes closed as though he were asleep. 'How ill is he? Can I question him?'

'No idea, I understand from the nursing staff that he's here for some tests. Best get the police doctor to see him first.'

Woods nodded. Younger than Anderson, Woods reminded Crane of an army officer in civvies, immediately recognised as police. He had that look. Hair sporting a short back and sides cut, with the air of someone uncomfortable with being out of uniform. Crane found the man prickly, but then so was Crane. Perhaps that's why they didn't really get along.

After the nursing staff confirmed that he could leave the hospital, Berry was arrested in connection with the murder of Owain Deans.

'What the fuck?' he said, as a uniformed constable put on the handcuffs. 'Owain is dead?'

'That's what I just said,' intoned Woods.

'But I've done my time!' It seemed Berry just couldn't shut up. 'This has got to be all wrong. I want a solicitor.'

'We'll arrange one for you down at the police station,' agreed Woods.

Then it dawned on Berry. 'Oh dear God, I'm not going back to prison, am I?'

As Berry was taken away, Crane could still hear him.

'Look, there's got to be some mistake! I haven't killed anyone!'

Crane knew Berry would appear before Aldershot Magistrates the following day and the police would press for a custodial solution instead of bail, as Berry had already absconded from the probation service whilst he was on licence.

The Magistrates would have no other choice but to remand him in prison until his trial.

CHAPTER 36

Jason Boult was speaking, but John Berry wasn't sure what he was saying. He seemed to be living in a glass box, where noises were distorted. As though he were underwater at the swimming baths. Then his mind suddenly cleared, and he snapped back into the present. He wasn't swimming, he was under Winchester Crown Court, waiting for his case to be called.

'Sorry, Mr Boult. Can you say that again?'

Boult sighed. He still had that Adams apple thing going on and Berry took care not to be mesmerised by it. 'I'm trying to tell you that the trial is presumed to last 2 to 3 days.'

'Is that all?'

'Yes, well, there's not much to be said, to be fair. It's up to the prosecution to prove that your act of stabbing Owain Deans caused him to die five years later, which means that you're charged with murder.'

'This is such a fit-up,' Berry complained. 'How can they charge me twice?'

Boult sighed. 'You're not being charged twice, John. You were convicted of GBH then. And this is murder, now.'

'How many witnesses do they have?'

'Only three.'

'And how many do we have?'

'None.'

'See that's the thing. How come we haven't any?'

'Because it's up to the prosecution to prove a causal link, not us. And, of course, Owain Deans is dead, and we can't argue that he isn't.'

Berry looked suspiciously at his solicitor. He'd never trusted the man and wasn't sure that he trusted him now. 'And you're sure they're not fitting me up?'

'Absolutely sure. What they are doing is perfectly legal.'

'You're up, Berry.' They were interrupted by a prison officer entering the cell. There was no more time for conversation. The show was about to start. Sighing, John Berry stood and allowed himself to be handcuffed to the officer.

'See you upstairs,' said Boult.

Once 'upstairs' Berry could see a packed courtroom. It seemed everyone wanted to catch a glimpse of the man who had tried to murder someone twice. He felt like a circus exhibit. As though he were a woman with a beard. Or the Elephant Man. He could see the Prosecution Barrister in his finery, conferring with colleagues. There was that army bloke, Crane, with his entourage. DI Wood and his lot. He could see members of the press, notebooks at the ready. Oh, and there was the court artist, pencil poised, looking right at him.

They all looked so confident. Looked as though they belonged. Not like him. He was like a fish out of water. He was outnumbered. Outgunned. He was going down.

ALDERSHOT NEWS

A lodger who stabbed the owner of the property he lived in, will serve a life sentence after his victim died five years after the attack.

John Berry, who had already served four years of an eight-year sentence for wounding following the initial incident, is now serving life imprisonment, after the death of Owain Deans.

A jury at Winchester Crown Court found Berry guilty of murder within an hour of retiring to consider its verdict. Sgt Major Crane from Aldershot Garrison called it a 'tragic and unusual case.'

Berry was originally convicted of section 18 wounding following the attack at the house they shared in Aldershot. Angry with Mr Deans, Berry armed himself with a large kitchen knife before stabbing him. One large, deep stab wound to Owain's abdomen was said to have been 'life-altering'.

Expert medical evidence showed that medical complications linked to his original injury caused his death. Mr Deans died from septicaemia.

DI Wood from Aldershot Police said: 'From the day that he received the serious injury until the day that he died, Owain Deans was never free from the great damage that had been done to him. Berry intended at the time either to kill him or at least cause him serious harm and this stab wound eventually lead to Deans's death.'

Berry was ordered to serve a minimum sentence of 19 years minus time served.

The victim had spent a great deal of time in and out of hospital. He underwent a number of operations and over the years had a considerable amount of medical treatment. A post-mortem concluded that the cause of death was septicaemia caused by complications from his ongoing medical condition as a result of the original stab wound and the necessary surgery.

Major Martin a Home Office Pathologist said, 'The deep stab wound that John Berry inflicted on Owain Deans was a life-threatening and life-altering injury. From the day that he received the serious injury until the day that he died, Owain Deans was never free from the great damage that it caused him. It affected him on a daily basis and his quality of life suffered a great deal.

'Owain suffered many difficulties and eventually lost his life because of the devastating injury inflicted by John Berry, and I am pleased that justice has been served today for Deans and his family. My sympathies and thoughts remain with them. I am also grateful to the jury for their close attention to the complex medical evidence during the trial.'

In sentencing Berry, the Judge ordered that he serve the minimum tariff of 19 years minus the four years he had already served in custody, as a result of the sentence imposed for the wounding offence.

CHAPTER 37

Crane had no hesitation in calling everyone to the pub for a celebratory drink. Anderson, Dudley-Jones, Kim, Padre Symmonds and even Billy and DI Woods. They all gladly came and Crane got the first round in. He had a cider, Anderson a pint of mild, Billy wanted larger, as did Woods and Padre Symmonds. Kim wanted a soft drink.

'Hang on a minute,' Crane said, turning to Kim. 'A soft drink?'

She blushed. And the penny dropped.

'Bloody hell, you're pregnant!' he shouted.

'Maybe,' she smiled.

'Padre?'

'I know,' said Francis. 'I'm not sure I'll have the energy to keep up with kids, but I'll give it a good go!'

Crane's eyes filled with tears. His emotions had given him a side swipe. Swallowing down thoughts of his dead wife, Tina, he said, 'A toast to the happy couple, about to be a trio. Congratulations!'

'Congratulations,' everyone echoed and then all started talking at once.

They were pretty much a dream team, thought Crane, looking at them all. He was amazed to have such good friends and colleagues. He had friends he loved. A son he adored and a job he was enjoying more and more every day. He once again felt lucky and humbled that he had been given the opportunity to build such a life after the army. Both he and Kim had fallen on their feet.

Crane raised a silent glass to their fallen colleague, Owain Deans. By working as a team, they had all had a hand in getting Owain the justice that he'd deserved.

CHAPTER 38

Out with Daniel the next day, Crane was still thinking about the conviction of John Berry, and he grinned.

'What are you grinning about, Dad?'

'It's nice for you to have your mates around you, isn't it?'

Daniel nodded.

'Well, it's nice for me to have mine as well.'

'Who are your mates, then dad? I've got Jimmy from my class. David from football. Evan from swimming. And Clarisa from next door.'

Crane nodded. 'That's a good bunch of people you have there.'

'So, who are yours, Dad?'

'Billy, Dudley-Jones, Padre Symmonds and Kim, oh and Derek Anderson.'

'So, nothing's changed then?' said Daniel.

Out of the mouth of babes and children thought Crane. 'No, Daniel, you're right, nothing's changed.'

As they climbed out of the car Crane's mobile rang.

'Ah, good afternoon, Sgt Major. Bevins from Aldershot police here, sir.'

'Hi, Bevins. What can I do for you? We won, remember, so surely there's nothing wrong.'

'Ah, well, it's just that a body has been found.'

Crane's stomach sank. 'And?'

'Well more of a skeleton. It was found in the canal.'

'What has it to do with me?'

'It looks like he's been shot in the head.'

'Again, what has that to do with me?'

'We also found a set of tags lodged in the mud underneath him.

Looks like he was a soldier. So, we might just have found another one of your cold cases.'

To be continued...

COLD WATER

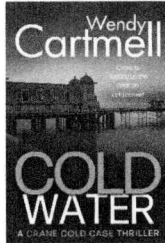

When a skeleton is found in the Basingstoke Canal, a man appears to have been killed by a single gunshot wound to the head, which was found floating nearby. DNA tests indicate the body is Sgt Green, a soldier from Aldershot Garrison, a soldier's whose child, Max, had been assumed abducted at the same time Sgt Green disappeared. It was generally thought at the time that Green had absconded with his child. But that assumption now appears to be wrong. Why was Sgt Green killed? And where is Max?

A NOTE FROM WENDY

Dear Reader

Welcome to the world of Sgt Major Crane and associated books!

It all started with the Sgt Major Crane crime thrillers, then the Crane and Anderson serial killers and now the Sgt Major Crane cold cases. There is also a supernatural series featuring DI Jo Wolfe, a cozy mystery series set in Muddlebay, three Emma Harrison mysteries, oh and a couple of haunted house novellas.

If you enjoyed the book, would you please consider leaving a rating and/or a review. This helps inform other readers when they are choosing what to read next and allows them to discover the world of Sgt Major Crane.

Thank you for reading my books, it means more to me than you'll ever know.

Best wishes

Wendy

By Wendy Cartmell

Wendy Cartmell is a bestselling Amazon author, well known for her chilling crime thrillers. These include the Sgt Major Crane mysteries, Crane and Anderson police procedurals, the Emma Harrison mysteries and a cozy mystery series, set in Muddlebay. Further, a psychic detective series has been written, the first of which, Touching the Dead has been followed by six further books in the series. Finally, the haunted series is a collection of ghostly happenings in buildings or objects. Just click the covers to go to the book pages on Amazon.

Sgt Major Crane crime thrillers:
kindleunlimited

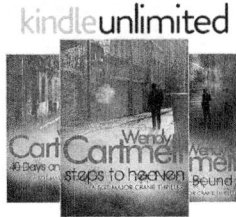

Crane and Anderson crime thrillers:
kindleunlimited

Emma Harrison mysteries
kindleunlimited

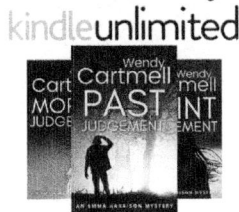

Supernatural suspense

Cozy mystery

Cold Cases

Printed in Great Britain
by Amazon

47861854R00066